9 40323924

Beneath the Skin

Sandra Ireland

Polygon

First published in Great Britain in 2016 by Polygon,
an imprint of Birlinn Ltd.

West Newington House
10 Newington Road
Edinburgh
EH9 1QS

www.polygonbooks.co.uk

ISBN 978 1 83697 361 1
eBook ISBN 978 0 85790 331 0

British Library Cataloguing in Publication Data
A catalogue record for this book is available on request
from the British Library.

Typeset by 3btype.com
Printed by TJ International Ltd, Padstow, Cornwall

To my mum, Ella Forbes Redfern

I

The girl hands him a mask. It has the colour and texture of an eggshell, carefully blank, with two slits for eyes. He can't take his eyes off the eyes.

'Don't worry.' The girl smiles at him. Her badge says 'Melissa'. 'Take your time getting started. Don't think in terms of creating a finished product – it's the symbolism that's important.'

She's pretty. Earnest. Pretty earnest. What makes a lass like that get involved with a bunch of damaged squaddies, handing out stuff like it's a children's art class? What was she trying to achieve? Walt didn't buy it, all this art therapy bullshit, but his doctor had referred him. He was supposed to be grateful.

He sits and looks at the mask. *You haven't a clue, mate. You haven't a clue what goes on in my head.* You can walk away from the war but the demons walk with you, every step of the fucking way.

'Any ideas? No?' Melissa tilts her head to one side. She has a sweet face. 'There are examples around the walls from my last class, if you want to take a look.' It's as good an excuse as any to get up from the desk, to keep moving. The guy opposite is really getting stuck in, mixing a palette of tomato-ketchup red. Walt shivers. *Too close to the bone, man.*

He begins to slowly circle the room. This trendy arts complex is on the outskirts of Newcastle. Steven and Natalie dropped him off and have gone to the Metrocentre for a couple of hours, leaving the wee ones with Mam and Dad. He has the feeling it had all been orchestrated before he'd even decided to do this.

The place has a print studio for kiddies and pensioners with nothing better to do. Now it's full of wounded soldiers mixing paint and dabbing with thoughtful brush strokes.

'Have a look at the walls,' Melissa reminds him.

The masks on the walls are horrendous. If that's what people are carrying around in their heads they're seriously fucked up. He remembers that painting he'd seen once when he was on R&R in Oslo. *The Scream*. He remembers the round 'O' of the mouth, the bulging eyes. The nose reduced to two slits in a jaundiced mask of a face. He'd been whole, back then, not really on speaking terms with anguish.

Some of these masks are split in two, asymmetrical horrors with bleeding eye sockets and black words carved into the cheeks, the skulls. REMORSE. GRIEF. GUILT. PAIN. HATE. Some are painted bone-white, others yellow, sulphurous like the devil. They have stitches for mouths. They seem to close in on him like a screaming gallery of the dead and dying. They are the faces he sees in the night, the demons that live in his breast pocket. His knees weaken and the sweat begins to pool in his lower back.

Oh God. No, not now, not here. His heartbeat thumps in his throat, strangling him. He turns to Melissa. 'I can't do this,' he says. 'I can't do it.'

And she says, 'It's okay. Take all the time you need.'

He finds himself outside in the cool air. There's a café bar with patio tables. He wants to sink down onto one of the cast-iron chairs and light up a fag, but instead he walks unsteadily through an archway and across a timber bridge. He can't control it: the panic, the flashbacks. It's happening a lot. No one ever speaks of it, the way you go off to war cocky and reckless and come back all messed up. They haven't come up with a therapy that can give you back your innocence.

The arts centre is set in its own landscaped grounds, with a rippling stream and a woodland walk for the school kids. He moves into the cool drabness of the trees. Stopping beside a weathered oak, he lays a hand on it. The tough bark grows warm under his skin. The tree reminds him of his mam's garden.

He's not sure how long he's been gone, but Melissa looks relieved to see him. His hands are full and he drops his collection of twigs and bark onto the worktable and smiles for the first time that day.

'Got any glue?'

2

He had arrived in Edinburgh without any clear notion of what he was going to do next and ended up in Stockbridge, of all places. He'd had an aunt in Stockbridge, and recalled dutiful visits to a grim tenement with a horsehair sofa and a teapot shaped like a crinolined old lady. The place now had the feel of a bustling but trendy village. An entire basement culture seemed to be going on – bars, coffee shops and designer boutiques sitting snugly below pavement level. There was no plan. He, who had coordinated incisive military manoeuvres, was flying blind. The train from North Berwick had terminated in Edinburgh, so he'd got off, hitched his rucksack higher and wandered out into the city. Its heavy brewery smell left him longing for a beer, but it was too early, even for him. Tossing a pound to the tired piper at the junction of Waverley Bridge and Princes Street, he'd headed north, slantwise across the New Town. Down and across, down and across, like a board game; pushing his luck at the pedestrian crossings, finding himself looking up at St Stephen's Church. It sat at the junction of two roads, where the cobbles made the walking hard.

From there, he'd carried on into Stockbridge, not quite sure where he was going, what he was doing. At least it was dry; he could sit in the park, make a plan. In this tourist city it wouldn't be hard to find a cheap hostel for the night.

He shared the pavement with smartly dressed professionals grasping to-go coffee cups, dog walkers, elderly shoppers with bags of groceries, young parents with prams. They all looked busy, content. He kept to one side, head down, slipping past them all. He fingered the loose change in his pocket, counting the coins. It wasn't a lot, but he had a few notes tucked into the bottom of his bag.

At the next corner, he turned left, and came to a sudden stop when he spotted a sign lashed to some basement railings: 'Wanted: Assistant. Must be STRONG and not SQUEAMISH.

Stone steps led into an abyss, and as he speculated about what was down there, in the dark, the weight of his rucksack threatened to yank him off balance. The straps were digging into his shoulders, squeezing his chest and stopping his breath. He shrugged off the pack and wedged it in the sharp turn of the stair. Down below, he found a dusty window and a closed door; the sign above read, simply, 'Stuff It'.

He pressed his face to the window, scrubbing at the grime with the cuff of his jacket. Yellow eyes stared back at him and he shied away, almost stumbling over an antelope's head on a wooden shield leaning against the door jamb. Then he spotted a grey cat curled up in a basket. He prodded the creature gingerly with the toe of his sneaker. Nothing.

A bell jangled as he opened the door. Floor-to-ceiling shelves of sparrows and magpies and rooks dominated the space, and there were tiny, delicate things too – butterflies pinned to beams, a sharp-nosed shrew beside the till. The cold air smelled of death, but clinically so, as if all the decay had been leached out.

A golden eagle dominated the single window, a chink of daylight accentuating the curved beak and the subtle crest of the wings. He'd never been so close to such a creature before. It was huge, magnificent, its power preserved in death. He stroked its feathers, dared it to blink, to tilt its head, just a fraction. The hollowness inside him grew deeper.

Turning to face the counter, he found himself looking at a

beheaded stag. Wasn't there a joke about how fast the beast was going when he hit the wall? It didn't seem that funny now. The counter was an old-fashioned jeweller's cabinet with a glass front, but in place of diamond rings lay a grinning crocodile on a bed of green velvet.

'Yes?' A woman emerged through a curtained doorway, revealing herself almost magically. He wasn't sure what he'd been expecting, but she'd taken him by surprise. She seemed too bright, too young, too fragile to be in a place of so much death. His eyes lingered on the fine detail: long hair the colour of wheat, birdlike bones in her wrist as she tucked a strand behind her ear. She was wearing a stained white jumper and high leather boots. The only bit of shape about her that Walt could see was a slice of denim-clad thigh. He struggled to remember why he was there. Ah, yes. The sign. She looked like the sort of person who would write in those jagged creative strokes.

'You want an assistant?' he asked.

She looked surprised. 'Do I?'

'The sign.' He made a slight turn towards the door. 'On the railings? I was just passing. I–'

'Oh, the *sign*.' She nodded quickly a couple of times. 'Are you strong?'

He was over six foot. What did she think?

He didn't like the way she was looking at him. Women usually responded to him in a certain way. He seemed to tick the right boxes; not too thin, muscular. He had longer-than-regulation, thick dark hair and a nose that had been broken once or twice. He sported a bit of stubble but was otherwise clean. He changed his socks, smelled of soap, and he knew how to slant his smile and crinkle his eyes for maximum effect. But this woman was looking at him like none of that registered, like she was seeing underneath, to the bits you're not supposed to see.

'I'm strong,' he said. Her cool grey eyes were peeling back his skin, counting his ribs. His stomach clenched.

'Are you squeamish?'

He glanced around at her dead animals. 'I'm here, aren't I?'

'Name?'

'Walton. Robert Walton. But you can call me Walt. Everyone does.' He shot her his best grin and stuck out a hand, but she only looked at it with interest.

'Walter? Walter Potter is my favourite Victorian taxidermist. He was a genius at creating anthropomorphic dioramas. Taxidermy isn't for wimps.'

He didn't know what she'd just said but he felt vaguely irritated. 'It's Walt, not Walter, and do I look like a wimp?'

'I'm Alys,' she said. 'You'll do.'

3

The first thing he encountered on entering Alys's house was a massive polar bear. Stuffed, naturally. It stood guard at the bottom of the staircase, upright like a man, teeth bared, paws extended, claws like daggers. It had a faraway look in its eye. Resigned, Walt thought. He asked Alys if it was one of hers, but she'd just looked at him blankly. 'We call him Shackleton.'

He'd been invited in for coffee, to seal the job deal. He hadn't been sure whether that would entail coffee, beer or the slightly darker something that Alys's eyes hinted at when she looked at him. Did she want to shag him or stuff him? Anyway, they came up out of the basement and into the house above, an old Victorian building with red-brick edges.

The kitchen was large, high-ceilinged, with an L-shape of shiny units taking up one corner and a table in the centre, a big old farmhouse one with six chairs. It was piled high with boxes, newspapers, unopened bills; the usual kind of kitchen crap that no one ever bothers to shift. They had a drawer for it at home, in the pine kitchen dresser. His mother used to scoop the accumulated junk into that drawer and if you lost anything you'd have to empty out the whole shebang.

Alys made him coffee. He'd have liked a beer. She told him her sister lived with her. Maura, her name was, but everyone called her Mouse. She didn't say who everyone was, or how she'd got the nickname, just that Mouse had a little boy of eight, William, and they lived in the attic. He was trying to listen like he gave a shit, but mention of the attic did bring to mind an image of a batty old dame in a moth-eaten wedding dress.

'We call it the attic, but actually it used to be the servants' quarters,' Alys was saying, adding, 'We don't have servants now. Unless you count Mouse.' He just looked at her, trying to read her expression.

Alys went off to find the sister, leaving him standing in the kitchen, but that was okay; he was better standing. He could see the foot of the grand staircase from there, and a portion of the hall. It was good to be within sight of an exit route.

The coffee was rank. Leaving his post briefly, he upended it down the sink, which was full of dirty plates. On the drainer a stack of cold, sweaty foil containers suggested someone had a late-night takeaway habit; he noticed the menus beside the phone. His life had become so disciplined he wasn't sure how to cope with this kind of human frailty. On the far wall stood a Scandinavian bookcase crammed with a smörgåsbord of titles: *An Artist's Guide to Anatomy*; *Thomas the Tank Engine*; *Hollywood Wives*. Three cat bowls sat in a row beside the bookcase. He preferred dogs himself.

He thought of Scoff, the dog he'd adopted on his last tour: a proper old mutt, part collie, part terrier. Loved a game of football and the chocolate they got from home. He remembered one of the lads saying you shouldn't give them chocolate, because of the theobromine. It kills dogs, theobromine. But Walt had laughed and said there was more chance of the mutt stepping on an IED than getting chocolate poisoning. Poor old Scoff. He should have given the dog more chocolate.

There were footsteps on the stairs. He positioned himself in the doorway, nearly filling the frame. Mouse paused when she saw him, the top of her head level with the polar bear's ears. Light came from somewhere high up, a landing window perhaps, and dust motes danced like fleas in the air above the bear's head. She looked about the same age as her sister – Walt guessed mid-twenties – but seemed more down to earth than Alys. She was wearing some shapeless woolly sweater and it was hard to get an impression of her figure, but he liked her hair; it was fiery. Alys drifted down the stairs after her sister. They were talking about him, heads together, hands on the banister. He was struck by how similar their hands were; long arty fingers, blunt nails. They were whispering. He couldn't hear what they were saying, but Alys's tone was abrupt. Mouse looked straight at him, once, and the way she looked made him stand up straight. Alys merely glanced at him, her expression untroubled, that of a person used to getting her own way. Their argument had nothing to do with him, he told himself. He was just passing through. Eventually, Mouse threw up her hands and stomped down the remaining stairs.

Alys turned, shooting a little victory smile in Walt's direction as she brushed past him. She cleared a space for herself at the table, pushing aside a bundle of envelopes and multicoloured junk leaflets. Mouse followed.

'Alys, there's William to think about.'

Alys raised a shoulder. 'It's *my* house.' There was a little cold snap between them then, a distinct icy blip. Mouse, still ignoring Walt, stalked to the sink, hauling up her sleeves, and turned the hot tap on full. The water bounced over the grimy cups and plates. Alys, humming softly, began to unwrap something from layers of newspaper. Walt moved to lean silently against the worktop, observing Mouse's profile as she attacked the washing-up: the nipped-in mouth, cold eyes. She turned off the tap with an angry twist and glared at her sister's back.

'You haven't even asked for a reference. He could be an axe murderer . . . or a rapist or a paedophile.'

Alys finished unwrapping. She was holding something across her two hands like an offering. Walt could see a lolling head and a black-tipped tail. Something dripped onto the table, something that may have been blood. He fought down the familiar nausea. Whatever it was, it was very dead. He cleared his throat and nodded at Alys. 'I'll need a reference too. Your sister could be dangerous.'

His joke fell flat, disappeared without trace. The weight of the house seemed to be settling around him. Just go, he told himself. Just get out. It's a shitty job anyway.

Mouse remained mute. There were tiny lines of strain at the corners of her mouth, as if she spent a lot of time gritting her teeth. Her prickliness was starting to piss him off.

'Look, I'm just a regular guy looking for work. I can get you a reference like that.' He snapped his fingers. 'I'll give you a number and you can contact the MoD.'

'You're in the military?' Mouse looked even more suspicious.

'Was. Rifles. Came out last year.'

Mouse dried her hands on a tea towel and searched amid the debris on the worktop. She found an old biro and a notepad, which she thrust in Walt's direction.

'Write it all down – the number to ring, your full name, rank and all the rest. She won't check you out, but I will. If you've got anything to hide, bugger off and leave us alone.'

Their eyes locked. He took the pen and scribbled on the pad.

4

When the smoke cleared he found himself looking up at the sky, blue as a bairn's blanket. This is heaven, he thought. I've died and gone to heaven. But the blue was so bright it hurt his eyes and when he tried to close them that hurt too, as if the skin of his face had shrunk. The noise phased back in: yelling and gunfire, someone groaning.

He was groaning. It woke him up, and he lay there staring at a plain white ceiling. Breathing hard he counted the cracks around the light fitting. His mouth was dry. He was afraid to swallow in case he tasted blood again. The skin beneath his clothes was damp with that dread sweat that prickles like iced water. Every pore was alert to the contours of the room, the temperature, the sounds; his inner radar scanning for clicks and creaks, sinews taut as tripwires. He couldn't place himself. He was in no man's land, dangerous territory where your oppos can't hear you shout. Reaching for all the things that he couldn't live without; his firearm, his ammo, radio, the clumsy comfort of his helmet. All vaporised. His hands found only jersey and cotton and lightweight civilian things.

After an eternity of two seconds he realised where he was, lifting his head from the soft pillows. He felt groggy and disorientated, his heart thudding painfully.

Real life was happening outside the window. It was open a crack and the nets were shifting; he could hear endlessly shrieking seagulls and the ripped-rubber roar of taxis on cobbles.

He swung his legs to the floor; he hadn't even removed his shoes, not intending to fall asleep, just to lie down for a second and process this new twist his life had taken. He limped to the window, cursing a new sore spot that had sprung up on his knee. He'd have to check that out later. Beyond the window, everything was grey: the street, the tenements, the light. A thin mist was hanging over the place. If he pressed his burning forehead to the glass he could just see the top of the flaky railings that led down to Alys's basement studio. As his body began to settle he thought over the series of events that had led him here; just a few days before, though it felt like longer.

It had been so easy. No references, nothing; he couldn't quite believe his luck, if luck was the right word. Screw that. He didn't believe in luck any more; it was all about surviving, and doing what it takes to survive. So here he was, getting paid cash in hand by the most unlikely taxidermist he'd ever met. Come to think of it, he'd never met a taxidermist before, and Alys had been quick to point out that she was so much more. She was an *artist*.

There was an intimacy about the dim studio, the way they were, a man and a woman, standing alone among the lifeless. It was only natural that they would eye each other up, all casual, picking up on the little sexual clues. By the end of their first conversation, he had felt that she'd warmed to him. She'd even offered him accommodation, a room in her house, above the studio. Though he still didn't like the way she looked at him. He pulled back a little from the window. The paint on the sill was white, glossy and squeaky clean. His fingers brushed against some trinket on the ledge. It was a piece of artwork, obviously created by Alys. An old bird's nest, a lovely piece of architecture, round and solid, the dip in the centre lined with down and moss. Alys had reimagined it, adding a rat nibbling on a broken egg. Another three pearly eggs nestled in the crook of its tail. It was surreal and slightly repulsive. He supposed he'd better get used to it.

Alys's house was squeezed between student tenements on one side and a low-roofed dance studio on the other. Standing on the pavement in front of it, you'd think it was a doll's house: the six steps up to the glossy green door, the sash windows and the dull red brickwork. Walt imagined taking the front off, exposing all the rooms and their dark little secrets. You'd see Mouse reading in the attic, William building Lego; Alys's plain white bedroom. The first-floor bathroom, big enough to dance in, with the claw-foot bath tub and the heavy showerhead in its cradle. You'd be able to hear the burbling of the old boiler, the purring of the four cats in the airing cupboard and the faint creaky respiration of the house itself.

It was the sort of house that breathed a sigh of relief after dark. You could imagine the rafters sagging like Victorian ladies loosening their stays. Already Walt was learning the sounds of the place. The letter box shivered in the wind; the seventh and ninth steps dipped and groaned as he walked up the stairs. His bedroom door had a worn brass knob that never quite caught, causing the door to fly open in the middle of the night.

There were cold spots on the landing, cracked panes, flaking paint and cobwebs that no one could reach. If Alys's house were a doll's house, you'd probably just replace the front and tiptoe away.

Alys had four cats. Five, if you counted the stuffed grey one in the basket down in the basement. He'd been formally introduced to *that* cat on his first day, when they were locking up for the night. Though he had since learned that Alys never really shut up shop, but roamed around the building like a ghost.

'This is Hector. I put him outside during daylight but I bring him in at night,' she had said, cradling the basket under her arm.

Walt had tickled the oblivious feline chin. 'So is he . . . glued to the basket?'

'Certainly not.' She had snatched the basket away. 'I would never glue him into place. He's free to . . . be.'

'Be?'

'Hector *is*.' The cat had continued to gaze at some distant horizon. Almost like a regular cat, but for the dust on its eyeballs. Walt's shudder had taken him right back to the desert, to open-eyed corpses half buried in sand. Why the fuck was he putting himself through this? He must be crazy, getting caught up with someone who found dead things so appealing.

Walt stepped away from the window and stretched out his stiff leg, noting the dull ache around his knee. The days so far had been uneventful. He spent a lot of time doing admin. Alys never seemed to answer the phone or reply to emails. He had busied himself wading through a backlog of enquiries, chuckling at the odder requests – 'How much would it cost to mount a pine marten?' – and contacting potential clients who were either used to Alys's eccentric business style or had given up and gone elsewhere.

In the evenings, when he had the chance to review the day, he thought about Alys a lot. He supposed she was eccentric, although some might have a different word for it. Her attention was on a timer; her eyes would slide away as you talked to her, her thoughts already on a different loop. People seemed to bore her, including her sister and nephew. She yawned when things got emotional, like she couldn't be arsed with complicated stuff. Hunger, cold, boredom – these were the things that preoccupied her. Anything heavier, like William crying over some playground spat, or Mouse stressing over an unpaid bill, had her heading for the hills – or rather, the basement. Even the cats weren't petted like regular cats. She stroked them as a chiropractor might, fingertips second-guessing their internal workings. And the cats were passive with her, draping themselves over her arms, wiping their chins against her face. It made his skin crawl, the way she clutched them to her body, letting their tiny paws knead her flesh like the hands of a suckling baby.

The cats were a ragbag of colours; black, two tortoiseshell and a fat white one, called Alaska, who was deaf. The other three had old women's names which Walt couldn't quite recall; Abigail or Enid or something. They all responded to a generic 'Cats!' and a toe up the backside when Alys wasn't looking. Mouse, on one of the few occasions their paths had crossed, said primly, 'I take it you're not a cat person, Robert?' No, he'd said, he was a dog person. Definitely dogs.

Mouse was always so formal with him. He'd told her twice to call him Walt, that everyone did, apart from his mother. Maybe, being a mother herself, it was all she could manage.

He wanted to know why Mouse was called Mouse, but it didn't seem the sort of thing you could ask without having some kind of dialogue first, and Mouse made it obvious she didn't want to start a conversation. She did her best to stay out of his way and the child, William, was ushered quickly up the stairs between spells of school or whatever. Mouse worked in a pharmacy, so sometimes the lad was looked after by the dance teacher from next door. Alys wasn't babysitter material, Mouse said.

The way Mouse hustled William past him in the hallway was the way his sister-in-law, Natalie, had been at the end. His niece and a nephew were younger than William, and he loved them both in a vague sort of way. It was pointless trying to remember birthdays, he was always away, but he made sure he bought them huge presents when he got back: giant teddies, Scalextric, computer games. Like Mouse, Natalie had subtle ways of letting you know you'd messed up: a tightening of the mouth, maybe, or a clipped word or two. When the wheels really started to come off, he'd seen her whispering to Steven. After that, Steven would put on a certain face when Walt offered to babysit. 'It's okay, man. We don't have the money to go out anyway this week,' he'd say, or, 'No worries, kid, Natalie's mum's already offered.' Stuff like that. And Natalie would squeeze the kids closer, as if he might infect them with the crazy bug.

Anyway, the cats ignored him, unless he had a can opener in his hand. They prowled every surface, lurked under the table and raided the bins. Every bin in the house seemed to contain a collection of feathers and unclassified bits of gore – fur, claws, tiny bones as sharp as needles and endless streamers of bloodied kitchen roll on which Alys had wiped her hands. Mouse had told him that part of the taxidermist's skill lay in stripping the skin from the carcass, never opening the body cavity. Someone should have told Alys.

Mouse had also revealed, with a certain pride, that Alys had sold a piece to a famous American collector. She'd told him all this breathlessly, as she scrubbed the downstairs cloakroom sink with bleach. Walt watched dried-on smears of blood disappear beneath her cloth, and realised that Alys paid her sister to clean. How convenient, he thought, having someone there to clean up your mess.

5

He trudged down the stairs to the basement, butterflies dancing in his belly. It wasn't the work that made him uneasy – though it wasn't exactly enjoyable – but the atmosphere of the place. He felt claustrophobic, shut in with all those dead animals. The air was cold and heavy, a constant pressure on his neck and shoulders, prickling his skin.

Thankfully, his new boss didn't seem to care if he went missing from time to time, so frequent fag breaks, a chance to come up for air, helped him get through it. He'd draw out each cigarette for as long as possible, his skin crawling at the thought of once again descending the stone steps into the basement.

He shook his head, told himself to get on with it. He'd been lucky to get this job; it meant cash in hand and a place to stay. He took a deep, final breath of the outside air and stepped back inside.

Later on, while preparing to finish up for the day, he decided to ask Alys about the mess. It was a taxidermist's job to preserve, he thought, so why all the scraps?

'I do a bit of butchery on the bodies,' she said. 'I eat them.'

His stomach went cold. 'You eat them?'

'It would be a waste not to, wouldn't it?' She was working on a gerbil, leaning over her workbench with the lamp pulled down. She was lost in her own little bubble of light, leaning in, her nose inches from the scalpel. Even from several feet away, Walt could smell the blood. He could detect it, these days, unfailing as a mother scenting her newborn. He watched her for a moment, mesmerised by the deft, restless action: little feathery shaving strokes, shucking off the skin to reveal a poor, pink mouse-shaped blob. The sort of thing cats leave behind.

He said it again. 'You eat them.'

'Yes. Well, not these, obviously!' She held the remains up to the light, flesh the colour of a bruise, glistening. 'How lovely it is . . . When you cut into an animal, the colours . . . Purple, silver. Beautiful.'

He had felt that he was intruding, that she was speaking as a lover might.

'Our best bits are beneath the skin.' It was no more than a whisper, but that whisper cut through him like that icy blade, and his own skin shrank in on itself, the hair on the back of his neck bristling. The cold spot in his belly began to swell and he clapped a hand to his mouth.

She put down the corpse and giggled like a child, picking up the bloodied skin to fit it over two fingers like a glove puppet. Affecting a high, silly voice, she made it dance after him.

'Hello, Mr Walt! We're having pheasant for tea. Will you join us?'

Walt was already heading for the door. The curtain wrapped itself around his face and he fought it. Sand was choking him, getting into his eyes, his nose. Blackness closed in on him, but he could still smell blood. He could still hear Alys laughing.

Time seemed to slip and jolt, and he was back on the battlefield. He spun away, in slow motion, one hand gripping the back of his neck, trying to anchor himself, and when that didn't work, he crumpled to the floor. His hand came away from his skin slick with sweat. Or was it blood? Painted masks danced in front of his eyes. He was in the desert, exposed, falling to his knees in the sand. He felt the grains between his fingers, white hot, blistering. There were bodies in front of him, and parts of bodies. The smell made him gag, flies buzzing around his head

– he was going to be next. A medic, stooped over the nearest corpse, looked up at him with eyes of yellow glass. In his hand he held a bone knife, a fleshing tool. As Walt watched, the glass lenses burst; liquid dripped onto the sand like tears and it was Alys's face he was looking into. She smiled, face wet, licking her lips.

Hands gripped his elbow, lifting him. Had he screamed? He looked up. It was the child, William, grave-faced.

'Are you okay? You don't look okay.'

Walt scrambled to his feet. His top was damp, sticking to him. He wiped the sweat from his upper lip, slightly surprised not to encounter the grittiness of sand. 'I'm fine. I'm all right, kid.'

The boy stared at him sadly. 'They're dead, the animals. They can't feel anything any more.'

Walt snorted with humourless laughter. 'Aren't they the lucky ones?'

Mouse was drying her hair in the kitchen. The hairdryer was plugged into the socket beside Alys's freezer. Her eyes were half closed, hair fanning out around her, but when she saw Walt she flicked the off switch and everything returned to normal. Hair limp, eyes wary. That was her habitual expression, like she never knew what was coming in through the door.

'You look like you've seen a ghost,' she said. She unplugged the appliance, wrapping the cable round it with jagged little movements that reminded him of Alys.

'There must be fucking hundreds of them in here. Little animal ghosts living in the walls.' He pulled out a chair and collapsed into it.

'Stop it,' she said. 'Stop it. I'm just going to start the tea.'

'You know she uses a hairdryer?' His eyes were fixed on the one she'd just laid on the worktop. 'She uses a hairdryer to dry out the skins.'

'You can join us for tea, if you like.' Mouse was busy

somewhere behind him. He heard a knife on a chopping board and winced.

'I'll pass, thanks. I've lost my appetite.'

6

In the basement there was a patch of damp on the wall the shape of Africa. Alys hadn't even noticed it, but Mrs Petrauska, the dance teacher from next door, called by to say that the guttering had come loose at the back of the building. Walt had been sweeping at the bottom of the stairs at the time and only became aware he was being watched when her frame blocked out the daylight. She'd folded her top half over the railings that separated the dance studio steps from the abyss, her face a pale moon of displeasure.

They'd met for the first time in his second week on the job. In a rare, light-hearted moment, he'd thought it might be funny to tie some kind of animal to the railings, one of those stuffed monstrosities Alys wandered around with. He selected a little spider monkey and lashed it to the railings, but it had caused such panic among the tiny ballerinas that Mrs Petrauska had blazed out of the building to rant at him in Lithuanian. She had a death stare that reminded him of his old drill sergeant.

'The pipe, it is caput.' She snapped her fingers briskly, bringing him back to the present and making her bangles chime. He was a bit in awe of Evelina Petrauska. The spider monkey incident had really pissed her off, and they hadn't spoken civilly since. On the few occasions they'd come into contact, she would merely arch her strong black brows and freeze him with a glance. Her eyes were an uncompromising black, her lipstick dark as port. She could pierce you with a stare and you'd find yourself gazing at her mouth. It was unsettling.

She dressed in intriguing layers, mostly black, which flapped importantly around her like graduation robes. She wore leggings with flat pumps and no socks, not even on the coldest days, so the exposed bits of her feet and calves were always a raw chilblain pink. She reminded him of the figure drawings they made you do in school, rendering all the body parts down to their most basic shape: oval. Everything about Mrs Petrauska, her face, her eyes, her droopy breasts and her large feet and hands, was oval. He guessed she was a few pounds heavier than she'd been in her prime, but she still had the grace of a dancer. She always stood with her feet turned out, the way ballerinas do, and when she talked her hands joined together and seemed about to float upwards in some kind of arabesque.

Walt cupped his hands around the end of the broom and leaned on it. She was deigning to talk to him now that she wanted something fixed. Did she think she could just snap her fingers and he'd fix it?

'Caput in what way?'

'It come away from the wall. She, Alys, she never checks the building. Last winter we had rats because she never put the bin out. She *beprotiškas*.' She whirled magenta nails beside her temple. 'You tell her from me, come away from all that . . . that . . . bunny butchering and come fix her caput pipe! And you – you're even more *beprotiškas* for working there!' She sniffed and flounced off back to her ballet class.

'There's a damp patch on the back wall. Do you want me to take a look at the pipes?' Walt asked.

'What pipes? What damp?' Alys replied.

'The rain's been seeping into the wall because your pipe is broken.'

'Eh?' She shrugged, changing the subject immediately. 'I haven't really shown you round the basement, have I?'

They were standing in the shop, her studio. It was cold in there.

A weak sun struggled to make it through the grimy window and past the golden eagle. A bare electric bulb provided light, the long flex swaying slightly even though there appeared to be no draught. He felt a hundred pairs of eyes on him: the stag, the eagle, the tiny field mice on the table in the corner. Alys was upbeat, smiling at him as she pulled aside the curtain for him to pass through into the back room. She didn't draw back like most people would, to give him space. She took up the space and he had to brush past her, his clothes coming into contact with her clothes, static blooming between them. Had she felt it too, that tension? Was she coming on to him? She followed him through into her workshop, and his spine tickled. He felt awkward around her, too conscious of his own movements, of her nearness.

A battery of lights took up the wall where her bench was situated: anglepoise, spotlights, floor lamps, all projecting fat silver cobwebs onto the walls, and she liked to be there in the middle, preying on her animal corpses: chopping and stretching, teasing and manipulating. Like a spider, she was luring him in here. The last place on earth he should be working in was a dark cellar. He'd served his time in foxholes and trenches, in places where the light didn't shine. Away from her glowing web the basement was full of shadows.

There was a door at the back, which was locked. He'd tried it, inquisitively. He'd seen her with keys but hadn't been quick enough to ascertain where she kept them. It was small details like that that kept you alive.

'Go on then. Give me the guided tour.' He swept his arm back towards the unlit bowels of the basement. Her answering grin made something jump inside him. She brushed past him, black feathers from the workbench fluttering after her like ghost birds. There were keys in her hand, although he hadn't seen her take them out of a drawer or a handbag. Did Alys even own a handbag? It didn't seem likely.

He followed her reluctantly to where the lamplight didn't

reach. He wanted to smack on a switch somewhere and flood the place with electricity, but she was confident in the dark. She pressed her back against the locked door, as if there was a surprise party waiting behind it and she wanted to ramp up the excitement. He could see the rapid rise and fall of her diaphragm under the white shirt, and he wanted to touch her, to experience some human contact. But she was already in another place, in her head.

'You remember I mentioned Walter Potter?'

The name conjured up an elderly gardener or a retired minister. 'Brother of Harry? Beatrix?'

'Walter Potter is my inspiration!'

'Right. Cool.'

'He created tableaux of animals; kittens, frogs, birds. Victorian whimsy. Come and see.' She whipped around to unlock the door.

Even before the light went on, Walt felt some presence tickling the nape of the neck. It was the same feeling he'd had many times in Afghanistan: an instinct on entering a space and feeling the weight of it, knowing that something else was there, unseen, sharing the same air. That instinct had saved his life more than once.

But when light flooded this space he realised there was no threat here. The absence of life alarmed him – shelf upon shelf and row upon row of lifeless bodies, glassy eyes, reaching paws. It was almost too much to take in. There were birds, of course, tiny ones: tits and robins and finches, spiky with claws and beaks and ruffled feathers. There were rats in tuxedos playing cards, stoats smoking cigars. A trio of toads dressed as Chelsea pensioners. But worst of all were the kittens. They took up a whole shelf on their own. It appeared to be a wedding party, complete with a Siamese vicar in a clerical collar. The 'bride', an emaciated tortoiseshell, was dressed in Gothic black lace and the groom, sporting a black top hat and a piercing in his little pink nose, was frozen in the act of placing a tiny ring over one of her unsheathed claws.

Revulsion flipped over in his belly, like something horrible waking up. How could she think this was okay? It was barbaric. He took a deep breath, fighting the urge to gag.

Alys was smiling with pride. 'Like it? It's my homage to Walter Potter.'

'It's a bit . . . creepy,' was all he could manage, but she wasn't listening. She skipped forwards as if to embrace the wedding tableau, carefully plucking at this and that. The vicar held a prayer book. The best man was a ginger kitten, painfully young, wearing a snazzy bow tie and bearing a velvet ring cushion. Alys flicked its tassels.

'Walter Potter completed *The Kittens' Wedding* around eighteen ninety. It had twenty kittens in mourning suits and brocade dresses, most of them made by his daughter Minnie. This is my take on it. I've gone for a more punky feel, you see.' She rearranged the bride's black lace veil. The kitten wore a startled expression, as if it couldn't quite believe what had happened to it.

Walt felt like his mouth, too, was hanging open. He cleared his throat. 'I kind of get the birds and stuff, but . . . kittens?'

'*The Kittens' Wedding* actually ended up in America,' Alys continued, as if he hadn't spoken. Off she went, like she was quoting from a book. 'It was sold for over eighteen thousand a few years ago. But it would fetch a lot more now. Taxidermy is the new black!' She giggled. 'Potter's whole collection was broken up and sold off. Damien Hirst wanted to save it for the nation but it wasn't to be. Scandalous.'

Like he gave a shit. The place was oppressive. The sick feeling wouldn't let go of him and he wanted to get out. His voice sounded rough, even to him. 'Who would buy this stuff?'

His words fell on deaf ears. He shivered. The place was on the chilly side, no doubt to preserve the art, if you could even call it that.

'I'm working on something else at the moment.' She came back to him, conspiratorial. He realised she was holding one of the wedding guests in her hands; a black-and-white feline maybe six weeks old at time of death, attired in a kilt and ripped leather top. 'Potter's most famous tableau was *The Death and Burial of Cock Robin*. It took him seven years to create and he used nearly a hundred birds, some of them now extinct.'

'I'm not bloody surprised.'

Alys's gaze narrowed a little. Was he pushing it a bit too far? 'Anyway,' she continued, 'I aim to do my own little tribute. You know, some of Potter's birds actually cried glass tears.'

'Tears from a glass eye? Incredible.' He wasn't sure if she got his sarcasm; she was in her own little world, clutching the kitten to her chest like a teddy bear, rubbing her face against it, just as the living cats rubbed their chins against her skin. She was looking at him in the way felines look at you when they suss out you're a dog person. Like they can turn you with a single blink of their uncanny eyes.

He had to get out of there. Turning on his heel, he blundered through the door, back into the main part of the basement, suddenly longing for heat and light and air. He didn't turn back to see whether she was following him, but he knew she'd be laughing.

7

Stuffed kittens? Walt was still turning it over in his mind at lunchtime, as he sat on the basement steps nursing a mug of tea. Where was she getting the kittens? They couldn't be all roadkill, could they? There wasn't a mark on them. It reminded him of that movie, the Stephen King story with the undead cat and characters you weren't too sure about until the end.

He chucked the dregs of the tea into the dust and patted his breast pocket for his cigarettes. He couldn't get Alys's expression out of his head, the way she'd looked when she'd rubbed the kitten against her face. It was as though she couldn't tell the living from the dead.

She appeared suddenly at the door. 'Are you having a fag? Light one up for me.'

No 'please' or 'thank you'. Still, he pinched a cigarette between his lips and sparked up his lighter. He drew on it heavily and passed it over. 'I've never seen you smoke.'

'I'm a social smoker.'

Social? Alys? She had to be kidding, but her face was impassive. He sneaked a look at her profile as she drew on the cigarette. He liked how the action made her cheeks hollow. It was erotic. There was something about her that he found appealing, though he usually didn't much care for women who were stick thin, like she was. She looked as if you could blow her away like thistledown – but not without a fight. You'd find her clinging on firmly by her fingernails. She was a battler, and he liked that.

Not his kind of battle though, the earthy, destructive type. Her battles were of the cerebral kind. You could see it behind her eyes, the constant shifting dart of the creative impulse.

She took another slow drag on the cigarette, and he narrowed his gaze. She made him feel jumpy, like he wanted to have a go at her, and that worried him. He liked being around lasses, usually. They were a calming influence. But not this one.

'The world is full of folk bumming ciggies,' he said. 'Folk who never buy any and then look down their noses at those who do, like they're weak and needy. It's a power trip.'

'Are you weak and needy?' She pouted a thin blue stream of smoke into the air. It sounded vaguely flirty when she said it, but he turned his face away from her, and she changed tack. 'So what's it like, where you come from?'

He shrugged. 'Pretty remote. A village surrounded by . . . nothing. The moors, the Cheviots, the odd salmon river.'

'Sounds quiet. Is that why you joined up?'

'I suppose so. Home was too small, the road to Newcastle too long. I was bored. Me and my mate Tom enlisted together.'

'Join the army, see the world.'

'Parts of it.' He stubbed out the fag beneath his heel and stood up abruptly. He didn't want her to ask about Tom. 'I'll go and have a look at this gutter.'

She considered this for a moment, before drawing a key from the back pocket of her jeans. Was that where she put the storeroom key once she'd tucked up her dead kittens for the night?

'You can get into the garden that way.' She nodded to an odd, wedge-shaped wooden door he hadn't noticed. The area outside the studio was a weird collection of angles. If you stood at the bottom of the steps that climbed up to the pavement, you were almost underneath the stairs that crossed the gap to the glossy green door of Alys's doll's house. The oddly-shaped garden door had been made to fit, lopped off across one corner. Walt reached out to take the key from Alys. It was still warm from her body, and the warmth somehow slipped down into his belly. Don't even think about it, he warned himself. No good could come of *that*.

He wrestled with the gate. Was she still watching him? The skin on his back grew hot. The gate creaked open and he eased through, closing it firmly behind him. A vague sense of relief washed over him as he loped around the side of the building. The grass was long, starred with daisies; a few chipped terracotta flowerpots were stacked against the wall.

Round the back, he checked the downpipes. They were of the old, heavy sort, layered with wartime green paint and rust. When he tipped his head back, the height of the building was dizzying; the system of pipes branched out, clinging like cast-iron vines to the brickwork. The connecting brackets were embossed with what the antiques pundits would no doubt call 'period motifs'. Very creative, the Victorians. He pulled experimentally at one of the pipes. A bracket at shoulder-level had come adrift, leaving a hole he could poke two fingers in. A bit of plaster should sort it. He must ask Alys where the nearest DIY shop was. He could fix it in ten minutes.

His body was starting to settle, after the horrors of the basement. A final, almost imperceptible shudder ran through him. Breathe. Just breathe and let it go. He let his gaze wander along the base of the wall, making mental notes as he went. This would be the back wall of the basement, although most of it was below ground level, obviously. There were a couple of vented bricks there, and . . . a tiny window. He couldn't remember seeing a window in the basement. There definitely wasn't a window, because it was so damn dark. Was there a window in the locked inner sanctum, the place of stuffed kittens? He couldn't recall, but he'd got the impression of wall-to-wall shelves.

He peered closer. The window was at knee-level. He stooped and wiped a circle with his hand, just as he'd done that first day, when he'd first come across Alys's studio. He could see nothing but the kind of blank darkness that makes you want to pull away.

He turned his attention to the pipe again. The drain cover at the base of it was blocked with leaves and muck, which wouldn't be helping the damp situation. He scraped it away with the side of his foot, encountering resistance. The grate was spiked with bits of debris: leaves and stiff twigs, or were they . . . bones? Little, brittle rat bones. And those weren't leaves. It was vegetable matter of some kind. Peelings, perhaps. Onion skins? Who would be out here messing around with onions and whatever the hell all these bits were?

He wished he'd brought tools. He usually had a penknife about him but he must have left it in his room. He didn't like being unprepared. Nor did he like to leave a job undone. Little details bothered him; leaves and twigs, or whatever they were, bollocking up the drains bothered him. Carefully, he began to prise up the cover.

He saw it happen in slow motion; felt the sickening crunch a split second before the heavy iron grid slammed down on his thumb, and then he was on his knees, cradling his hand against his gut; his body clenched tight against the pain. Blood pulsed in the screwed-up darkness behind his eyelids. Something alarming and visceral took over: sand choking him, disembodied voices in the static. In his chest he felt the tell-tale throbbing heartbeat of the helicopter coming to get him. The pain was so deep he couldn't feel it any more, was riding above it, floating somewhere in the dust clouds and he heard them calling . . .

Robert. Robert!

They never called him Robert.

That's what brought him back. They never called him Robert but there it was in a panicky kid's voice. *Robert!* He dragged in a breath. Did he have sweets on him? They all wanted sweets, the kids. Or pens, or footballs. He squinted upwards, and the eyes staring down at him were blue. That jarred too, because he knew they should be brown.

'Robert, are you okay?' A hand jostled his shoulder, and he

was suddenly back where there was no sand, no heat, no sound other than the screeching of the gulls. He came back to an ordinary grey granite afternoon, finding himself kneeling in the dirt like a prize fucking idiot, hugging a bruised thumb.

'Does it hurt?' Blond hair, blue eyes, gazing at him in alarm.

'No, bonnie lad. I'm fine. Just let me get up.' Walt winced as he got clumsily to his feet. Every time this happened, it took longer to snap out of it, as if a part of his brain was still in that other land, unwilling to come back and fight this different kind of fight. William was watching him silently. He raised a smile for the child's benefit. 'It's all right, son, I just hurt me thumb.'

Carefully he unwrapped his fingers so they could both inspect the damage. William wrinkled his whole face, brow, nose, the lot, as he checked out the blackening nail and the swelling flesh. The digit was like a black grape, but luckily there was no blood.

'Ugh. Is it broken? Can you wiggle it?'

'Yeah, I can wiggle it,' Walt declared without checking. He tucked the injured hand into his armpit. What was the lad doing here anyway? His system began to click back into gear. 'Shouldn't you be at school?'

The youngster was dressed in civvies, faded jeans and a hoodie.

'I was feeling sick this morning, so Mum left me with Mrs Petrauska when she went to work. I don't really like Mrs Petrauska. Her eyes are too black and she smells of garlic, but she lets me watch David Dickinson. I like David Dickinson. "Cheap as chips."'

'You're weird.' Walt eyed him suspiciously. 'And you don't look sick.'

'You do. Your face has gone white.'

An awkward silence ensued. He didn't know how to be around kids any more. He'd been used to short, frantic bursts of playtime with his niece and nephew, hyping them up with unsuitable presents and too much sugar until Natalie's tight expression warned him off.

Mouse's son was small for his age. What was he – seven, eight?

An ad man's dream, the sort of blond cherub that could sell anything from sugar frosties to paint; a kind of golden child with two smiley parents, a Labrador puppy and a fishing rod. But when you *really* looked at him you could see the tarnish; skin peeling where he'd chewed his lip, shadows under his eyes. He looked like a kid who'd stayed up late with one too many violent computer games. He was watching Walt, waiting for some kind of adult exchange, and when it didn't come, he seemed to make a decision. Gripping Walt by the wrist, he began to lead him back to the front of the building, carefully, as you would a docile but unpredictable bullock.

'Come on, I'll get you a plaster.'

Walt followed obligingly. He wanted to point out that a plaster probably wouldn't cut it, but instead he said, 'It's okay. Alys is there. Shouldn't you go back to Mrs Petrauska's? She'll be wondering where you are.' William didn't look round. 'Alys doesn't know where the plasters are.'

Of course she wouldn't. Not babysitter material, Mouse had said.

They passed Alys sitting on a low stool in the doorway, smoking, the white cat curled up on her lap. She looked at them without interest, until the black thumb was produced for inspection. Then her eyes lit up.

She dropped the cigarette and jumped to her feet, brushing off the cat. It skulked away into the shadows to groom its fur. Alys moved towards Walt, a little too close, cupping his injured hand in hers, her touch insubstantial. He smelled smoke on her scalp. His damaged hand lay in hers, upturned, like a dead thing. She was gentle but it was an odd gentleness. He tried to ignore the pain, which was threatening to burst out through the mangled tip of his thumb. It was nauseating, but he would never admit it, would grit his teeth against exposing it, because he'd experienced so much worse, witnessed so much worse. To admit to any kind of hurt was a betrayal.

She was probing the base of his thumb with her fingers, nipping his bones and ligaments like a dog that wouldn't stop biting until its teeth met. He pulled his hand away. He thought she looked vaguely amused. Whatever that expression was, it didn't seem appropriate, and the young lad, down by his elbow, saw it too and his eyes shuttered. 'Could be a fracture of your distal phalange,' she said. 'It happens. But more likely to be severe trauma to the pulp surface. Did you know the distal pad of the human thumb is divided into a proximal and a distal compartment? The proximal is more deformable than the distal and allows the thumb pad to mould around an object. Lucky, really.'

'What the hell are you talking about?'

'Well, there's a bit of "give" in your thumb. They're hard to break. You'll probably lose the nail though.'

'How come you know so much about thumbs?'

'I've stuffed plenty.' She grinned when she saw his face. 'Not any human ones. Yet.'

'I still think you need a plaster,' William said.

8

The last night on patrol is always the longest night. If you're going to give in to your fears it will be then, in the dark hours, between sundown and the welcome roar of the Hercules that's going to take you home. Your psyche is jumping with tales of those who bought it on their last day. That's got Sod's Law written all over it: to dodge bullets for six months and then stumble into an IED tripwire on the final night of your tour. Nobody mentions it, but the thought is there, buzzing around you like a fly. Prayers are imagined a little louder, charms fingered for luck. Walt's amulet is a Saint Christopher medal that belonged to his granny.

Your whole system is tuned to the slightest movement, the faintest sound. Shadows trick you; the air is sticky with tension. Your training kicks in and you realise there's a certain balance in dodging bullets, a law of averages. You can fire back. You are a leveller. It's the IEDs that scare you shitless. You're fighting ghosts.

That's how it was for Tom – a roadside blast on his final night; the night before he was due to go home to Sara and the kids; due to stride off the plane and engulf them in bear hugs. The army medics radioed it in as 'significant damage'. Walt could see that Tom wasn't going to stride anywhere in a hurry. Two mortars had detonated, making a mess of Tom and little Deano, a young squaddie of eighteen, first tour. Both of them were conscious as they loaded them into the Chinook. The lad was screaming for his mother and Walt would never forget how Tom reached out to him with his one remaining hand. Come on, bonnie lad. You'll be home before you know it. By the time Walt and the rest of the unit had made it back to base in the armoured vehicles, Tom was dead, had slipped away into the dark night high above the desert. The young lad had survived, minus his legs. Walt was still trying to decide who was the lucky one.

9

The pharmacy was a family-run independent a fifteen-minute walk from Alys's house. Walt was unsuited to walking with a child and it was a long fifteen minutes. His gait was all wrong for a start; it was impossible to match it to William's. He'd been proud of his military stride, the way it covered the terrain, the way it got him noticed on Civvie Street. Old soldiers bought him pints and clapped him on the back; girls gave him the eye. But nothing was scarier than feeling the kid's hand worm its way into his at the junctions. There was a warmth to it, a comfort he'd thought he could live without. At the second set of traffic lights he started to get paranoid. Were people looking at him? Speculating? An adult male with a kid that wasn't his. Did they know? William tugged on his hand – 'the man's at green, we can go now' – like a little guide dog.

The boy kept up a steady stream of chatter, as if his words had been stoppered up for ages and Walt was the only one who could listen. The lad was a magpie: a collector of other people's thoughts, snippets of conversation and throwaway comments. He picked them all up and added them to the scrapbook in his head.

By the time they'd reached the pharmacy on Raeburn Place, Walt knew that the pharmacist was called Galen, that he kept a house in France and tiny scissors in his wallet with which he neatened his beard in the staff toilet. Mouse had apparently worked for him for seven years and was worried that he was becoming overfamiliar.

'What's overfamiliar mean, anyway?' William asked as they reached the shop.

Walt realised he was still holding the kid's hand and dropped it. It had gone all warm and sweaty the way kids' hands do. His own thumb was pulsing, getting worse the way a toothache does at the thought of the dentist.

'Sounds like he's an old lech.' Walt shoved open the door with his shoulder, nearly tripping over a girl who was unpacking a box of loofahs. She shot him a wide smile. Black-framed, ultra-cool glasses dominated her face.

'Who buys loofahs any more?' she said. As a chat-up line it didn't work, so she turned to the kid. 'Hi, William.' Her expression clearly said, 'Who's your friend?'

William jumped in with the story, polishing it up a bit: the downpipe; the ten-tonne drain cover; the thumb that was going green. His mother appeared suddenly behind the counter, managing to look shocked and annoyed all at the same time. Galen the pharmacist – the beard was neat salt-and-pepper – was hovering beside her shoulder, ready to jump in at the slightest hint of trouble. Walt judged him to be just short of retiring age; a trim figure in a dated brown suit. Mouse was wearing a navy coat over her white uniform. William repeated the tale again, but neither of them seemed particularly interested in an injured thumb.

'We don't really have a protocol for first aid,' said Galen.

'You shouldn't even be doing stuff like that. Did Alys ask you to do that? You should have said no, and *William* . . .' Here she paused for breath. 'You shouldn't be running around the streets. Does Mrs Petrauska know you're here?'

'Auntie Alys said she'd tell her.' William's face remained downcast; he was closely examining the floor, burrowing his toe into a hole in the faded lino.

'Ha!' said Mouse. 'As if Alys will remember to tell her! I'll check my phone. Mrs Petrauska is probably tearing her hair out and *you* are going to school tomorrow.'

'What about Walt's thumb?' William muttered. The kid had a stubborn tilt to his chin, like his mam. Galen began to stutter something about X-rays, 'just to be on the safe side'.

Mouse's anger seemed to melt a little. 'Show me your thumb.'

'It's after two, Maura,' Galen reminded her. 'You get away and I'll see to this. You'll be late.'

But she was already examining the bruised digit, her touch firm and warm – capable, Walt thought. He gazed at the top of her head. Her hair was as shiny as conkers in the clinical light, and he wondered what she was late for. The pain had subsided a little, but the nail was now the colour of charcoal, with a darker line across it where the drain cover had got him. Mouse made a low whistling sound. 'I wouldn't bother with the hospital. They won't be able to X-ray it while it's so swollen. I'd just keep it out of trouble for a while. You'll lose that nail.'

'I can live without it.'

She pursed her lips and nodded, releasing his hand. 'Take some ibuprofen.' She slanted her head towards the medicine shelves behind the counter. 'Galen will get you some. I have to go.' She glanced at William. 'Look, Robert – Walt – could you take William back to Mrs Petrauska's? I have to go somewhere and I'll be about an hour.'

'Are you going to see Granddad?' said William. 'Can I go?'

Mouse looked at Walt, and there was the faintest flicker of pleading her eyes.

He shrugged. 'I'll take him home. I'll get him something to eat and plonk him in front of the telly.'

William brightened immediately, though his mother looked nervous. Galen coughed discreetly from behind the counter. *Either buy something or bugger off.*

'It's okay. I *am* babysitter material.' He shot her his special lopsided grin. She was caught. She couldn't make a fuss here, in her place of work. Although she smiled politely, her eyes remained cold, as if she'd somehow been outmanoeuvred.

'Fine.' She fiddled with her coat. It was a soft blue woollen one with one of those tie belts, and she pulled the belt so tight she must have cut off her breath. 'William, behave. I'll be back as soon as I can.' And she stalked off to wherever she was going.

No doubt William would fill him in on the way home.

10

'Families are funny things,' said Alys. She worked in an intense sort of silence, her movements economical and deft. She'd been putting the finishing touches to a toucan, if toucans can ever look finished. Walt, attempting to tidy up around her, admired its glossy beak, which glowed in the spotlight like a Tequila Sunrise. The bird was destined for a new bar off the Royal Mile, and Walt was glad. It seemed like an escape somehow.

'Families *are* funny things.' He nodded in agreement, slowly wiping something sticky from the blade of a knife. Walt's role had turned out to be very fluid. As well as the endless admin, real live customers sometimes found their way to the studio, and then he would put on his best sales face and enjoy a bit of banter. It was a bit of light relief, actually. Alys didn't do banter. She couldn't stand him making any noise when she was working: no whistling, no humming, no jokes. When she was prising the skin from a dead carcass, he became a sort of squeamish theatre nurse, measuring solution, cutting wire, handing her the most wicked-looking tools he'd ever seen. And thinking, time after time, why am I doing this? What am I doing here?

Sometimes, when she came to the end of some project, like this toucan, she wanted to chat. It was like turning a pillowcase inside out, all the silky coolness giving way to the fraying, hidden bits.

'We get put in boxes,' she was saying. She ran a finger round the curve of the bird's beak. 'And we behave the way we're expected to. Look at Mouse. She hides from things. That's how she got her nickname. She hides and watches. She was always getting me into trouble when we were kids.'

He didn't know what to say, so fiddled awkwardly with bits and pieces on the workbench: a carpenter's pencil, a pair of spectacles. He wasn't sure what had brought this on, or where it was going. Alys had such a good memory. She used it as a weapon, an excuse to fester with old slights. He opened out the legs of the spectacles. They were the type of wiry, scholarly men's glasses that made him think of Galen. He'd never seen Alys wearing specs, but maybe she needed them for close work. He folded them up and replaced them, deciding it might be safer to change the subject.

'So what's the label on your box then? Tortured artist?' It was meant to be a joke, almost, but Alys didn't do jokes. She turned away from him, dusting her hands on her backside. He liked her backside, what he could see of it beneath the white shirt.

'If you're finished I have an errand for you to run,' she said over her shoulder.

He'd allowed himself a brief flare of lust; irritation quickly snuffed it out. He wasn't convinced he'd signed up to be an errand boy.

She disappeared into the shop. Her voice drifted back to him: 'But before you do, you can sweep up the fag ends outside.'

His lips twisted. She knew she had the upper hand and she liked it, and her liking it sent a depth charge through him that he couldn't ignore. He was not the submissive type, but he had to admit that Alys was getting under his skin.

She sent him to see someone called Moodie.

'He's a carpenter,' she had said. 'He's making something special for me, for my Walter Potter tribute.' She fizzed with excitement when she mentioned her work. He could almost see the shadows of long-dead birds flitting around in her head. She told him how she'd been planning it for ages, had designed the glass case and the backdrop herself and it was going to be epic. She'd even selected a title. Did he want to know the title? He said no, not really.

He had no idea whether 'Moodie' was a surname or a first name or one of those names that people use to single themselves out as unique. He'd once had a maths teacher who simply signed himself 'Fox' on his report cards. Years down the line Walt still visualised the man as a smart-arse ginger predator. 'If Robert expended as much energy on algebra as he does on forging parental notes he might yet go a long way.' He probably hadn't been thinking of Helmand Province.

This Moodie had a lock-up on Hamilton Place. 'Turn right, before you get to the river,' Alys had said. 'It's squashed between the public toilets and the bus shelter.' He figured it wouldn't take him long, and he didn't mind walking. Walking was meditative. He supposed it came from years of patrolling with blisters and an eighty-pound kit. Mind over matter. When he couldn't walk, in that black time, his head had been all over the place, like the black had got in there too.

Now as he walked, taking the same route as he'd taken with William, his thoughts turned to the little lad. The previous afternoon he'd taken the youngster home, as promised, while his mother went on her secretive mission to visit the grandfather.

'He lives in a *care home*,' William had confided. 'He can't remember stuff. Mum gets really sad about it because they stick him in front of the telly and don't cut his nails.'

'Typical.' Walt had automatically grabbed the child's hand as they'd approached the pedestrian crossing.

'I think that'd be okay though, don't you?'

'What, being in a care home?'

'Getting to sit in front of the telly all day.'

'Daytime telly stinks, believe me.' He could sense William looking up at him, and when he'd glanced down the kid was giving him the full-blown how-could-you-say-that treatment, with the wide eyes and the brows disappearing into his spiky fringe.

'But all the good programmes are on! *Cash in the Attic*, *Flog It!*, *Dickinson's* . . .'

'Are you for real?'

They'd stopped in the middle of the pavement. Walt quickly dropped the kid's hand as shoppers bustled past.

'I like all that stuff.' William stuck his lip out.

'You're ten years old, for Christ's sake.' He wasn't sure why this bothered him so much – surely the lad should be out climbing trees or something.

The pout thickened. 'I'm eight.'

'Eight. Okay.' Walt had turned to move on, with William trailing after him. 'When I was eight I was a tearaway, not a founder member of the David Dickinson Fan Club.'

'But I like collecting things. I'll show you.'

And he had. They'd gone in and turned on the telly in the cold green sitting room. Green was supposed to be a fresh colour, a colour of springtime and new growth, but in Alys's house it seemed mossy and damp. The long velvet curtains were always half drawn, like it was too taxing to make a decision either way. There was an upright piano in one corner, piled with dusty magazines, a sad-looking rubber plant and a stuffed owl. The owl looked like he'd rather be anywhere else. The three-piece suite, also green, had been shredded by the cats. The whole place smelled of cats. Opening a window might have helped, but he couldn't bear the thought of being invaded by the outside cold. There was a grand fireplace, inset with those tiles that depict toffs in hats and crinolined ladies. The grate was sealed off with hardboard. Maybe Alys trapped some of her subjects in there. It was a brave pigeon that flew down Alys's chimney. The television was, by comparison, a fairly new flatscreen. William had tuned in to his channel of choice before racing up the stairs to bring down his treasure trove.

Walt had collapsed onto the couch. He was unsure of what to do next. Could he knock off for the day, or was he expected to take over babysitting duties? That was surely not part of his remit, but he could hardly walk off and leave the kid in front of the telly. There were probably laws about that. The sounds of daytime TV washed over him. A grey-haired baker with twinkly eyes and a Mediterranean tan was turning steaming cakes onto a wire rack – 'and there you have it, carrot and cinnamon muffins. What could be easier?' If the kid didn't make it as an antiques guru maybe he could be a pastry chef. The credits rolled and the voiceover trilled, 'Next, David Dickinson discovers some real deals – but first the news headlines.'

Walt leaned forward. The music came on, loud and important – cut to a female presenter in a smart yellow blazer.

'Good afternoon. In today's news: Northumbria Police have asked for help in tracing . . .'

Suddenly, he was grappling with the remote control, pressing buttons wildly, willing the newsreader to disappear. Words punctuated his panic: *Missing . . . Extremely concerned . . . Any information, call this . . .* William returned at the very moment the channel changed. Walt flung away the remote, his heart banging in his chest.

'Hey!' William placed two shoeboxes carefully on the easy chair. 'David Dickinson is coming on!'

'But this is *The Simpsons*. Who doesn't like *The Simpsons*?'

'Me.'

'Look, kid, show me your wares and I'll stick Dick on again.'

'It's *David*.' William had dropped grumpily to the floor and prised open the first box.

Moodie's workshop was like a Tardis that had landed on the banks of the Water of Leith. As soon as Walt entered, the pithy stink of sawdust transported him back to his father's shed; his dad, methodical, silent, sanding something on the workbench. Pain twisted in his gut like a living thing.

Moodie appeared from somewhere out the back. An art

student by the look of him, got up in army fatigues although the worst action he'd ever faced was probably Edinburgh on a Saturday night. His pallor spoke of a heavy night on the ale, and Walt felt an unexpected flare of resentment. He missed that, the easy fug of his local, mates around him. Moodie's dreadlocks were bundled into an oversized knitted beanie, powdered with sawdust like an eighteenth-century wig. He wore those weird chunky spikes through his earlobes and his nose was pierced about five times. Walt found himself staring at the nose, and at the spider tattooed on the back of his hand.

'Alys sent me,' Walt muttered. It was like a bad spy movie. That first emotive sawdust rush had evaporated and the shop appeared squalid, with a sleeping bag in the corner and empty pizza boxes carpeting the concrete floor. A couple of twisted sculptures sat around, but not much other evidence of work. His dad's shed had been piled high with lovingly turned cherrywood bowls and trinket boxes; more than he could ever give away as birthday presents.

'So you're the assistant?' The guy's accent was London; chirpy. He even had a chirpy grin, which made Walt want to punch him. His temper was rising, he could feel the heat of it tightening on the back of his neck, tensing his fists. He stuffed them in the pockets of his jeans.

'Alys sent me to collect . . . whatever.'

The carpenter wiped his hands on his combat pants and set about rifling through the junk piled high on an old chest of drawers. 'Ah, Alys', he said. 'Quite a character, ain't she?'

'Aye.'

Moodie glanced at him. The 'whatever' had wiped away the grin.

'But she's a powerful artist, man. Powerful.' A pile of magazines waterfalled to the floor and he kicked them away with a well aimed boot. Ex-army boots. Walt's gaze stabbed into his back, but the youth continued to chatter, regardless. 'She could give

Damien Hirst a run for his money. I keep telling her – you need to go large. Fuck the kittens, go for a giraffe. A giraffe embryo in a glass tank. Where did I put the thing?'

Army boots? You've got to be kidding, Walt thought, gazing down at his own feather-light trainers. Comfortable and practical, the physio had said. And this goon was wearing army boots.

'If that's what you call art.' The words tasted bitter on his tongue and the carpenter turned round as if they'd scalded him.

'What, mate?'

'Modern art is all a bit too Emperor's new clothes for me.'

Moodie's lip curled. He looked vaguely ridiculous, standing there with a box of pop tarts in one hand and a roll of duct tape in the other. 'It's all about interpretation, mate.'

'So how do you interpret a bed, or a tent, or a cow pickled in aspic?'

'I'm pretty sure it wasn't aspic – and anyway, just because you don't like it doesn't mean it's not good.'

'Hiding in plain sight.'

'What? What do you mean by that?' Moodie slapped the things he was holding back onto the chest of drawers. The tape rolled off to join the magazines. Walt wanted to get out. The sawdust smell had lodged in his throat like smoke and he hadn't realised how cramped it was in here, how dark, but he couldn't stop the words spilling out, loaded words.

'It's what they say about people who are up to no good and taking the piss,' said Walt.

'Who says?'

'Anybody. The papers. They said it about those celebrities who were abusing kids.'

'What the hell are you saying about Alys?'

Walt had lit a fuse now, and he waited, watching it ignite, not quite sure how he'd got there, how he'd come in off the street and picked a fight with a guy he didn't know from Adam. 'I'm

49

just saying Alys has the label of being an artist, which means she can get away with murder.'

Moodie started flinging things about with more purpose, anger in every line of his spare frame. 'You're out of fuckin' order, pal. Where did she pick you up anyway? There's plenty youngsters wanting jobs.' He opened the drawer, grabbed something and brandished it in Walt's direction, like a weapon. 'I hope she knows what she's taken on.'

And when Walt realised what the object was, he whispered, 'So do I.'

II

He had to get out of the sawdust Tardis and away from this man who was looking at him as if he'd kicked a kitten. Alys was the one who did things to kittens. Moodie wasn't best pleased but he stuffed the thing into a Tesco bag and Walt stumbled off, following the river back to the bridge and trudging on, bending himself around afternoon shoppers. The day had turned dismal, threatening rain, and the old ladies had their brollies to hand, just in case. He was aware that he was walking in the opposite direction to Alys's doll's house. She'd be waiting for Moodie's masterpiece, but he needed to find some space, some lightness, away from elbows and voices and accusing stares.

He found the park. He'd known it was there, from his one recce when, after a few late-night beers in his room, he'd decided to go walkabout. He hadn't gone into the park, that time, not trusting himself. Just stood at the gate breathing in the cool dark and thinking of his mam's garden, and the scent of damp flowers and the leftover teatime smells. There was a pizza place nearby. He could smell garlic and pepperoni and it had seemed so ordinary, so life-goes-on; he'd turned round and gone back to his single room.

Now he went into the park, marched in, his steps jerky, and made for the nearest tree, an oak, wanting to lay his brow against it, feel the patchy roughness of its touch. But instead he did the civilised thing and sat down on a bench with a brass plaque to someone long dead and watched the squirrels and the ducks on the pond like a regular person.

He'd shoved the Tesco bag under the seat first, not wanting to be reminded of it.

It was the kind of park you'd call mature, a city oasis of big trees and gravel paths, formal shrubberies clipped back by council workmen in hi-vis jackets. The place was big enough to put some distance between you and your fellow man; the benches were widely spaced, the pond some way off. There were shiny black bins for litter and red ones for dog poo but there was still shit on the grass and Irn-Bru cans in the flowerbeds.

A watery sun had made an appearance for the kids coming out of school; there were a few of them in the park, running wild with their coats tied round their waists, and mothers with double buggies and the odd dog. The pond looked sluggish, a bit out of its comfort zone amid the tenements and the traffic, the sweet wrappers and the lager cans. Even the ducks lacked enthusiasm.

He spotted a couple with two under-fives, looking so like Stephen and Natalie that he almost got up. They had that obliviousness about them, cocooned in their own little world, their own family unit. The kids looked about the same age as his niece and nephew, although he couldn't exactly remember the numbers. Ella was just starting school in September and what would Jack be now – three? Down by the water's edge, the little lad kicked his football and was toddling after it in that stiff-legged, no-knees way you do when you're learning to walk.

Walt shivered. Someone walking over your grave, his mother would have said. Another little boy kicked the football gently back to the toddler. This lad was taller, thinner, with a mop of blond hair and a bright blue backpack. It was William, with his mother watching from a distance.

Walt automatically felt in his pocket for the button that was lurking there. He must give it back to the kid. It was one of his collectibles, fallen out of the box when he packed them all away. Walt had found it on the easy chair, a heavy silver button with a distinctive crest, an eagle, the kind you'd see on a vintage overcoat of some kind. He didn't know why he'd slipped it into his pocket; it had a military feel about it, maybe that was why. He really should give it back, before it became a talisman for his fingers in the dark of his pocket.

Mother and son began to walk towards him, and William spotted him first. The kid had that hyperactive after-school look about him, with the shirt flying out of his pants and his tie round his head like something out of *Lord of the Flies*. Grubby-faced, he had picked up a tree branch and was wielding it like a weapon.

'Walt! This is a sub-atomic space-alien vaporiser! BOOM! RATATATAT. BOOOOSH!'

Walt felt the blood drain from his face.

'William!' Mouse's voice was shrill with annoyance. The space-alien vaporiser continued to rain ammunition down on him until Mouse confiscated the stick and William stalked off in a huff. Mouse was unsmiling. Walt could see the hem of her white uniform below the blue coat, the coat belted so tightly it nearly cut her in half. Her hair was tied back and there were insomniac smudges below her eyes. She looked forlorn, like she needed a hug. The thought shocked him. His girlfriend, Jo, used to look like that when the kids gave her a hard day. She was a maths teacher; kids hate maths. It had been a natural thing, to jump up and give Jo a bear hug. But now he was too used to the cold touch of trees.

'Hi.' It was a safe enough greeting. He didn't get up and she paused in front of him. She had the height advantage and it made them both uncomfortable. William jumped onto the end of the bench, resuming his laser noises.

'William, get *down*.'

'He's grand.' Walt was glad, somehow, that the boy was doing boy things. He felt sad sometimes when he looked at William, without knowing why. It was the magpie thing maybe; all those treasures squirrelled away. Was that what kids did when they were insecure? It wasn't a great life for the kid, stuck in that house with an unstable aunt and loads of dead animals. He fingered the odd button in his pocket – but he didn't give it back. Instead he said, 'Good day at school, son?'

'It's school.' William shrugged and jumped down from the bench. 'We did art, though. I like that.'

'Taking after your auntie?' Walt smiled.

'God forbid.' Mouse flopped down beside him on the hard seat, as if reluctantly obeying a stronger force. She sighed and lifted up her feet, rotating the stress from her ankles. 'My boss is a plonker.'

Walt grinned; she glanced sideways and caught the grin, a small smile creeping in around the corners of her mouth.

'He is,' she said. 'He offered me a pay rise.'

'The bastard.'

She giggled. It was a nice sound, unexpected. 'He wants me to do more hours, be like a manager or something.'

'And you can't because?'

She nodded towards William, now searching for God knows what in the long grass at the base of the oak tree. 'I couldn't ask Mrs Petrauska to take him any more than she does. She already helps me out on school holidays and stuff. And you know he had the cheek to say to me, "Money must be tight, you being a single parent."' She adopted a low, ponderous Galen tone. '"My offer might help you get your own place." As if!'

'Why do you live with Alys?' The words were out before Walt could stop them. 'Why does she keep reminding you it's *her* house? Like you're the poor relation?'

Mouse looked at him with that tight mouth he'd seen before. She looked as though she wanted to tell him to bugger off, it's none of your business, but she didn't. She just got up and belted her coat even tighter and he was sorry then, because he'd been sort of enjoying the company. He missed conversation. You couldn't have a cosy chat with Alys.

'We have to be getting back. William has homework to do. What are you doing here anyway?' Her foot nudged up against the Tesco bag and they both looked down as if there lay the answer to the question.

Walt reached down and hauled the bag onto his knee. 'Your sister sent me to a charming man called Moodie to collect a prop for her latest *artwork*.' The last word lingered in his mouth. He ripped away the plastic bag with a flourish.

'Christ,' said Mouse. 'What next?'

12

'One mini gallows.' Walt handed the package to Alys, pleased that his hand was as steady as his gaze. She'd been threading wire through the skull of a magpie with a tiny pair of pliers but when she saw the bag she dropped them on the bench, falling on the package like a child on sweets. The Tesco bag fluttered to the ground.

'Amazing! Moodie is so *good!*'

'Is that how he makes a living? Designing miniature instruments of death and destruction?' He was joking, but not quite.

Alys brushed the dead magpie to one side and set the thing up on the workbench. 'Is it any worse than what you do for a living?'

'Did.'

She'd stopped listening. He moved to stand beside her, watching her in profile. There was a gluttonous look about her, and he couldn't resist asking about her plans.

'My piece will be called *The Death of the Wren*, my homage to Walter . . .'

'Potter. I got that. So what poor creatures are you sacrificing for this?'

She turned to face him then. The light in her eye had frozen to pale silver and she held the gallows like a crucifix. He wondered who was the vampire. He picked up the pliers from the bench, tested them against his thumbnail. The swelling had subsided and the nail was still intact, although it felt weird down at the base.

'Robert, I don't know if you're cut out for this job. I'm not sure you have an artistic temperament.'

The memory of the art therapy came back like a punch in the stomach. Traumatic memories can remain frozen in the body's central nervous system, the doctor had said. Was that why he felt so cold all the time, so cold inside? Like he'd eaten a block of ice.

A person will react to get through the experience, but the trauma remains unprocessed. The doctor had been an okay guy. Decent and earnest, just like Melissa the art therapist. They were all earnest, that was the thing. They all meant well, but they couldn't see inside his head, couldn't see the things he'd seen. Was still seeing. A person might get a sensory memory, like a sound or sight or smell, that is reminiscent of the trauma and all of a sudden they are experiencing it all over again. The past wasn't just with him, he was walking back through it, picking his way through a daily minefield of 'unprocessed trauma'.

Alys was still talking, half to herself. Her words didn't make sense. They seemed to be coming from some place inside the magpie's skull. Echoing. She was threading a wire through his brain and he could feel the cauterising heat of it and he felt himself slipping away. He was back in the art therapy place, back with Melissa, and his soul was the colour of a bruise as she held it up, glistening, in the light.

The mask is a masterpiece. A work of art so good it lifts his heart, and for the briefest moment he thinks, it's working, art therapy works and all the claptrap professionals might really know their stuff.

Oh, he'd listened to the introduction: 'Trauma often affects the non-verbal part of the brain, which is why many service personnel can't vocalise their emotions. Art therapy helps to translate feelings of loss, grief and pain to the verbal part of the brain, freeing them from the subconscious.' And it had. He has a sense of achievement, like he's been given a task and completed it, on time and to spec. It's a good feeling. And then Melissa, with her wide smile and her kind eyes, says, 'I can see what you've done, but let's see if we can unpick this.'

Unpick it? It's taken him almost the whole class to piece together his outside treasures, the bark and the leaves and the moss. He'd arranged them on the desk first, let the chill, musty smell waft him back to his mam's garden, to the pine tree where he'd hidden as a boy. Like most kids he'd taken safety for granted and that pine tree was the last place on earth where he'd been truly safe, anchored in its branches.

Painstakingly he'd transferred that feeling to the mask. It has thick furrows of bark for eyebrows, brittle scales of mulch and leaves for skin. It is a true mask, a camouflage of natural materials to hide behind, the merest of slits for eyes. He will be invisible behind that mask: Invisible Tree Man. Safe.

Melissa has spotted his expression and rushes on. 'When I say unpick it, I mean let's take a look at the emotions behind the mask, Robert.'

He waits. He wants to pick up the mask but it's on the table between them, and they're both leaning on the table, arms braced, as if it's a map of something, or a puzzle. He wants to hold the mask up to his face so Melissa can't see him.

'So let's have a think about this,' she's saying, slowly, as if she's laying out her own thoughts alongside his. 'What this says to me, Robert, is that you're still hiding. Where is the mouth?'

'I forgot about the mouth.'

'But it's important, the mouth.'

He can feel the tension ratcheting up inside him. This is the problem. This is why he's here, because he can't get a grip on the rage.

Melissa changes tack. 'What we have here is a depiction of something. We don't really see what's going on inside. Inside you.'

He thinks of the gallery, all the other guys' masks with the livid strokes and the burning colours and the awful blackness. He realises then that the tree couldn't save him. His mam's tree is no longer safe and he has nowhere left to go.

13

Walt blinked and refocused his gaze on Alys, the studio, the gallows, feeling the pliers still in his hand, reminding himself of his reality.

'I'm sorry, pet. You're the one with the vision. Tell me about it.'

Alys's face broke into a grin and he knew he was forgiven. She hugged the gallows to her chest. 'I'm inspired by the Irish legend of Clíona. She was otherworldly, dangerous. She lured young men to the seashore and watched them drown. A spell was cast to protect them, turning Clíona into a wren, and every Christmas Day she was fated to die by human hand for her treachery. Of course, that's the Pagan version. The Christians say it was the wren that betrayed Christ in the Garden of Gethsemane but either way the wren doesn't come out of it well.'

'No?'

'Nope. In Ireland they have the wrenboy tradition where wrens are hunted down and killed and hung on a holly branch and paraded from house to house on Boxing Day, although they're probably not allowed to do that now.'

'Where are you going to get a wren?'

She ignored him, holding aloft the gallows. 'Moodie made this out of holly wood. I'm going to create a tableau with the hanged wren at the centre of a rabble of small birds and animals. I might even have an old-lady hamster knitting at the foot of the scaffold!'

She giggled. Walt's face felt tight with disgust, but she didn't even notice. Perhaps she was right: perhaps he wasn't the right person for the job. 'It will symbolise cultural disdain for the innate Pagan power of the female.'

'Right.' She'd lost him again. He was thinking a long, cool beer would be good right about now. He'd shut himself in a room far away from Alys's artistic craziness, but then she turned and looked at him in that way she did sometimes, the way that made the pit of his stomach smoulder like she'd thrown a lit flare down there.

He had to speak, to break the spell. 'I went to the park.'

'I don't pay you to go to the park.'

'Mouse was there.'

'And?'

'She thought the gallows were a bit sick.'

Alys laughed, the sound strangely hollow. She snatched the little pliers from Walt's hand and tossed them at the magpie. They made contact with a flat *thunk* and the bird jerked as if galvanised back to life. A cold-water shiver dripped down Walt's spine.

'Mouse never approves. She's always been the same, creeping around, waiting for me to fuck up. As a kid she spent most of her life curled up – curled up in bed, curled up in the corner, reading a book. Never speaking, but watching everything. Hiding.'

'What was she hiding from?' The suggestion echoed in the dark basement.

Alys shrugged. 'Mice can turn. They pack a nasty bite when cornered. They're also a pest and hard to get rid of.'

Walt hesitated, uncertain whether she was serious or not. She didn't look amused. 'But you live together.'

'Not by choice. She got pregnant and the father didn't stick around. I'm the only family she's got left. It was my duty to take her in.'

Something didn't add up about that. What about the grandfather? The one in the care home? Dutiful was not a word Walt would have used to describe Alys. He began to think of other words: sexy, wayward, eccentric.

She was looking at him now, her eyes cool, calculating, unpeeling something inside him. 'Did you come here to talk about Mouse?'

'I came here to deliver your gallows.'

'Oh yes.' She picked up the wooden framework, caressed it with her artist's fingers. 'I like it. Look at the grain of the wood, the way it's finished . . .' Her voice dropped, catching with excitement, and there was something about the tone of it that vibrated in his groin. 'Ah, I have so much going on in my head . . . But you don't want to go there.'

It was the kind of thing he said to people, to keep them at arm's length, and for a moment he saw himself in Alys. She was like a mirror and he was drawing closer, close enough to see his reflection in her eyes, to mist her face with his breath, and when their mouths came together it seemed inevitable. It was tentative at first, a slow clinging of the lips, hands reaching out, finding. Alys dropped the gallows. It bounced off his leg but he didn't feel it; could only feel the soft, stained jumper, the narrow back. Her arms snaked around him, pulling him against her. She smelled of dead feathers and cigarettes. They pressed against the workbench and he was no longer sure who was instigating this, or who would be the first to draw away.

It was Walt, breaking the kiss but not the contact. They leaned together, lips damp, breathing hard. 'This isn't a good idea,' he whispered.

'It is.' She smiled and there was a new wickedness about her. Her eyes shone with it. 'Just don't expect to get paid extra.'

He pulled away from her. He picked the gallows off the floor and set it upright on the workbench, still tasting her, feeling her bones beneath his hands. He knew he wanted more. He knew he had to get away from her.

'I don't think we should go there again. And I really don't want to know what goes on in your head.'

Her smile was crooked. 'I think you do.'

14

Later, Walt went out to buy fags. A cold east wind had got up, bringing rain with it from the Forth. Not for the first time he thought about the grey Crombie overcoat he'd left in his wardrobe at home. He might have to buy another one if things didn't heat up. Or even a scarf, he thought, pulling the collar of his jacket up. Turning into Alys's road he took out his key. He was surprised to see a strange bicycle chained to the basement railings. Alys didn't have friends, and definitely not friends with bikes. Though it was an old-fashioned type, 'pre-owned', as they say in sales circles, and probably more than once. The saddle was dappled with drizzle. Curious, he let himself into the house. There were voices in the kitchen. He didn't have anything else to do, so he'd make himself a coffee and take it up to his room. His job was definitely part-time, sporadic. Sometimes he was sure Alys simply forgot he was there.

The table had been cleared, apart from the single place setting at the end. This was Alys's place, Mouse had warned him. It was always set for whatever meal she might turn up for. The tablemat was a plastic child's mat, with an orange cartoon fish, and her mug sat empty and waiting. The mug bore the slogan 'Taxidermists don't give a stuff '.

Mouse had a friend over for tea; they were sitting opposite each other, a white cardboard bakery box between them, and fat ginger crumbs on their plates, smears of butter cream. Walt recognised the girl from the pharmacy, the one with the geeky glasses. She smiled when he came in, the turn of her head quick, like a bird. Don't stay too long in this place, he thought, it's not a great place for birds. Her skin was pale and unwrinkled, like double cream, her hair blacker and shorter than he remembered. She was very animated when she talked, her nose wrinkling, dislodging the Buddy Holly frames. Mouse looked relaxed for once, her eyes picking up a spark from this girl. She'd melted a little, like her crisp shell was only sugar frosting and there was something luscious inside.

'Hi, I'm Fee,' said the girl. 'I saw you at the pharmacy.'

'Loofahs.' He went over and shook her hand. She had a good, strong shake for the size of her.

'Sorry, we ate all the cake but you can come and have a coffee with us,' said Mouse. He couldn't work out if that was the good mood talking or her usual need to do the right thing. They resumed their conversation as Walt filled the kettle and found a mug.

'I think you should go, Maura.'

'I'm not sure. It would be really awkward.'

'It's only a meal, you don't have to sleep with him!'

'Ugh, thank God!'

Walt swung into a spare seat, looked from one to the other. Mouse stared at her plate, but Fee laughed and said, 'Galen has asked her out!'

'What, the old chemist guy in the bad suit?'

Mouse rolled her eyes. 'He dresses very well, for his age.'

'For his age,' Walt repeated. 'What are you thinking?'

It was none of his business, obviously. You'd have to laugh, really, at the thought of those two together, Church Mouse and a guy old enough to be her father, jangling his money in front of her. She'd be lucky if that was all he jangled.

'He's sent her a friend request on Facebook and he has a house in the Dordogne.' Fee made big eyes, like this was the clincher. Mouse let out an embarrassed huff of a laugh.

66

'That's the worst possible reason to shag a guy, because you think he's got money,' Walt said.

'I would never do that!' Mouse's nose went pink around the edges. 'I wasn't even thinking of it!'

'I bet you were.'

'I wasn't!'

'You were. You were thinking, I'll latch onto this old bloke with money and a house in the Dordogne and all my worries will be over.' He was teasing her, but she'd turned angry; she couldn't meet his eye and when she did, eventually, he saw a sort of quiet desperation that he recognised. He felt sorry and didn't know how to tell her, but Fee had turned it all into a big joke.

'Galen's fancied her for ages!'

'How would you know? You've only worked there five minutes,' Mouse said.

'I do two days a week,' said Fee, sticking her tongue out. 'I'm a psychology student,' she added, in case Walt thought she was stuck in that shop, like Mouse, with no chance of anything better. That explained the spark. She was doing what Mouse longed to do. She had the life that Mouse had given up.

'And anyway,' continued Mouse, 'I'm not accepting his friend request. This is why I hate Facebook – it's creepy, everyone seeing what you're up to.'

Fee laughed and turned to Walt. 'You know she relies on William to help her with Facebook!'

'So?' He felt a pang of sympathy. 'She's right. She's got better things to do than post crap pictures of her sandwich on social media.'

Fee looked vaguely disappointed. William wandered in, still in his uniform, shirt untucked and carrying an enormous Lego spacecraft. He set it carefully on Alys's place mat and pulled out the chair with both hands. No one said anything when he sat down but Walt could see Mouse begin to fidget, with her teaspoon, her bracelet. He felt it himself, an indefinable uneasiness. He imagined Alys appearing, sweeping the Lego to the ground.

'Are you speaking about Galen?' said William. 'I went on the laptop, Mum, and checked your Facebook for you.'

'William! If I knew how to do it, I'd change my password!'

The boy giggled. 'I made you and Galen friends. Is he still an old lech?'

15

So he arrives home without Tom.

They should have been together, as always, anticipating the moment of touchdown, of coming down the aircraft steps and seeing their families waiting to greet them. Tom's wife would have been there, his little kids running to meet Daddy; and Tom lifting them, the Strong Man, one on each arm as they kissed his sunburned cheeks.

But there is none of that. The lads are subdued. There are funerals to go to, relatives to be phoned, respects to be paid. Walt knows he will go to Sara's first of all, they live near the base now, to tell her the things she wants to hear. No, he hadn't suffered. You don't feel the pain; your body goes into shock. Yes, he was joking around right up to the end. Same old Tom.

He catches the train back to Newcastle, slumped in the seat, angled away from the curious stares of the other passengers. There's something about the uniform that brings out extremes in people. They either want to shake your hand or give you a pasting. As the flat landscape speeds by, he rests his temple against the cold window and tries not to see Sara's tear-stained face in the ghost of his reflection.

His parents meet him at the station. His mother is pale, sobbing into a tissue.

'I can't believe it,' she says in the car for the tenth time. 'He was part of the family.'

She's sitting in the back, allowing Walt the honour of riding shotgun, the returning hero. He keeps his eyes on the road, on his father's dependable fists curled around the steering wheel. His mother has always stated the obvious. It's one of those endearing little quirks that irritate the hell out of him, like the way she carefully explains the ending of every movie even though you figured it out halfway through, and the way she repeats telephone conversations when you've been right there in the room listening. It's irritating and he doesn't need it, not now. Losing Tom is like losing a brother, but he doesn't want to keep hearing it. When he closes in on himself Mam gets all the more upset, hissing to his dad in the hallway: 'He's very quiet, do you think he's in shock?'

They hang their coats on the newel post as they always do, and dad makes tea. He's itching to get back to his shed, you can just tell. He's never been much of a talker and too much emotion really makes him clam up. He asks a few safe questions about the weather and the flight and when that angle dries up they sit at the table, listening to the dull tick of the kitchen clock. Mam has a turkey defrosting on the draining board.

'Life must go on,' she says fiercely. 'Steven and Natalie are coming over for tea, but I haven't said anything.' She nods her head towards the wall. He knows what that means. No family gathering is ever complete without Tom's elderly parents making the short walk from next door. Even when Tom had moved away to start a family, Bert and Maureen had always been included. Bert has a fondness for a good malt or three, and Maureen can talk for Britain, but nobody minds.

'I've been round to see them, of course.' Mam sniffs. 'But it's so hard. I feel so guilty.' The tears overwhelm the tissue and Walt doesn't quite know what's expected. He could do bear hugs. Bear hugs are friendly and safe, but if he clings to his mother now, he will come apart like the tissue. He knows all about the guilt. He reaches over and pats her shoulder.

16

'Let's do something normal,' he announced at the weekend, although he hadn't meant to stress the 'normal' quite as much. When Mouse turned to look at him – she was elbow deep in the kitchen sink again – he could see the word had found her.

'Normal? As opposed to what?' Her tone wasn't particularly friendly. She turned back to the sink to rinse the cutlery under the tap. She had on jeans and sloppy slippers and a grey cardigan that sagged at the back. She didn't look like someone desperate to escape.

He sighed. 'I just feel . . . redundant, I suppose. Alys told me to bugger off. She's been holed up in that basement for the last three days.'

She glanced around again with that little hitch in the corner of her lips, like when William said something funny.

'I thought she was quiet. Has she started on this wren thing?'

'Yup. She took delivery of a glass case the size of a kid's coffin and the gallows are all set up.' Mouse winced at the description.

'I was glad to get out of there. I get claustrophobia in that bloody basement at the best of times. Aye, I was glad to get out.'

He looked at William, sitting at the table with colouring pencils and paper, enjoying a Saturday morning breakfast of pop tarts. On school days Mouse cooked porridge, the comforting smell of it warming the kitchen for hours, but routine came undone at the weekends and Walt wanted a bit of that too.

'She's always like that when she's got a project on the go.'

Mouse turned back to the sink, shook water from a mug and placed it upside down on the drainer. 'She's driven. You learn not to take it personally.'

'I wasn't. How about a nice cappuccino on the Royal Mile?'

Mouse switched off the tap and turned all the way around, narrowing her eyes at him. 'Too far.'

'Rose Street?'

'Full of pubs.' They both glanced at the kid. It would have to be a threesome, of course.

As Walt searched frantically through streets in his brain, Mouse said, 'Ooh, I know somewhere with great cake, across the road.'

Walt grinned. Across the road would do. 'Great. Are you ready?'

'Some of us can't just drop everything and take off, you know. I have chores to do. And another thing . . .'

He hated sentences that began like that. Jo used to throw that one at him when they were arguing: *And another thing, that girl you were flirting with on Saturday night* . . . Weird that he should start thinking about Jo now. He'd been doing a good job of blocking her out.

'. . . so it's not a good idea, with all the cats about and . . . Robert, are you even listening?'

'I am listening.'

'You're not. What did I just say?' She glared at him with a touch of triumph. He hated that too.

They traded looks. He felt his face crease into a grin, and suddenly she was smiling too, although she tried hard to hide it.

'You were going on about takeaways. You thought I'd had a takeaway and not cleaned up after myself.' He stood his ground, laughing at her expression. 'Ah, you see, I don't miss much. But you're wrong, bonny lass, I would never leave a mess. The army knocks that right out of you.'

She opened her mouth to protest, but there was a truth there that she couldn't ignore.

'Seriously, there were open containers all over here.' She

gestured to the worktop. 'And the cats were up licking at them. Disgusting.'

He lifted his shoulders in an exaggerated gesture. 'Maybe it was Alys?'

'Oh no.' She shook her head. 'Alys would only eat Chinese if I ordered it. She won't talk on the phone.'

'Really?'

'Really. It's one of her things.'

'Maybe she had a change of heart. Whatever. It *definitely* wasn't me.'

Case closed. It took ten minutes but he managed to persuade her to leave her chores and be spontaneous. Then William had to be coaxed into his trainers and zipped into his coat. He wasn't finished his drawing, he said. And he hated coffee, and why couldn't they just leave him at home?

'Because you're eight and I'd be arrested.' Mouse pulled up his hood and the boy instantly flipped it down again. Walt sighed. He should have gone out alone, found a soft seat in a dim bar, people-watching with a wee nip in his hand. Now Mouse was promising carrot cake and lemonade and William was hopping from one foot to the other.

'I have to pee first,' he said.

'Go on then, and be quick. I need to change.' Mouse plucked at the cardigan.

'Maybe lose the slippers.'

'I'll lose the cardigan. Two minutes.' Mouse disappeared, leaving Walt in the kitchen.

The shut-in feeling was threatening to engulf him so he went outside, sat on the top step and lit a fag. The morning was cold with a hint of rain on the breeze. This was why he didn't date women with kids: the endless peeing and putting on of shoes and all the rest. He could have been sitting in a pub by now. He got to his feet as soon as they emerged, wincing at the pain in his hips. Sitting on cold stone wasn't a good idea, given the battered condition of his body. William's hair had been slicked down with water and he looked pissed off and whiney, and Mouse had to check her bag for keys and zip up her parka before they could set off. Walt walked quickly, trying not to limp, and the others had to run to catch up. He knew his mood was making Mouse nervous, but there was a perverse pleasure in seeing her flushed and breathless. It made her look alive.

'So where are we going?' He looked down at her, drawing heavily on his cigarette. She hated him smoking around the kid. She looked about to say something but he got in first. 'Everyone's allowed one vice, right?'

Her sudden smile caught him off balance. 'True.'

He grinned back. 'So what's yours then?'

'Oh, I'm still looking for mine.' The way she said it, the way she caught his eye and looked away quickly, made his heart twist. Whoa. Was she flirting with him? He frowned. No, he must have imagined it.

'We're going to Tea 'n' Flea,' William announced with an edge of triumph. This time Walt paused and stared at him. 'Tea and what?'

'It's a café and flea market,' Mouse explained.

Walt picked up the pace again. 'Kid's a bit of a squirrel, isn't he?'

'He's a nightmare. Most boys buy sweets. He spends his pocket money on stamps and coins and . . . rubbish!'

Walt felt in his pocket for the silver button and rubbed his thumb over the design.

The shop was painted bright blue. He supposed he'd passed it before, that night he'd gone out with a drink in him and ended up at the park gates, staring at the trees until the safe, clichéd smell of pizza nudged him away like the nose of a family dog. The shop had been closed that night, like all the other shops. Now there were trestle tables outside, defying the weather, stacked with old books and comics. Every time the door opened a bell rang.

Inside were actually two shops, sharing a damp lobby. Through a glass door to the left lay a labyrinth of dusty bookcases, packing crates and cardboard boxes stuffed with collectibles, curios and junk. To the right was the café, long and narrow, popular with the blue-rinse brigade. A refrigerated cabinet of quiche and salad took up most of one end, and along the length of the side wall a giant chalkboard advertised the specials in meticulous handwriting: mackerel and walnut salad; boiled egg and rocket panini; pastrami picnic loaf, whatever the hell that was. The place smelled of peppers and basil, overlaid with coffee. Sharp hisses of steam from the espresso machine competed with the soothing tones of Radio 4.

William chose a table by the window and they squeezed themselves in, Walt feeling like a giant on the spindly chair, the bistro table sagging under his elbows. The old ladies competed with each other, a torrent of voices with occasional crystal clear bubbles rising to the surface: 'Did you see that rain?' . . . 'It's not cold though, for April.' . . . 'That's Scotland for you – four seasons in one day!'

Send them out to the desert; see how they like the weather there.

Mouse caught his eye. 'What do you think?'

He looked about him, at the organic veg rack and the herb prints on the wall. It was a pine-nuts-and-sundried-tomatoes sort of place.

'It's okay. Reeks of vegetarianism.'

'You don't like vegetarians?'

'Don't trust anyone who doesn't like kebabs.'

'Walt!' She didn't know how to take him and it made him smile. There was so much warmth about her: her hair and her cosy jumpers, the way the tip of her nose went rosy in the cold, the glint in her eye when she was amused. She looked good when she thawed out.

The waitress came over, a student type with cropped brown hair and an Australian accent. Walt liked waitresses, shop assistants, nurses. With a bit of banter and his crooked grin, he could hold their attention for as long as it took to remember the man he used to be. But this girl didn't even look at him. The kid had her explaining all the soft drinks to him like he was ordering wine at Claridge's.

'What's cream soda like?'

'It's sort of creamy. Sweet. Hint of vanilla.'

'What about ginger beer?'

'You might not like that, honey. Ginger can be a bit sour.'

'Maybe I should . . .'

'Jesus, give him an Irn-Bru,' Walt said, rocking back in his chair. 'And coffee for us. And cake.'

The waitress and Mouse glared at him as if he'd just bitten the head off a hamster. He shrugged. 'We'll be here all day otherwise.'

They had cappuccinos and carrot cake, which was good: moist with a hint of cinnamon and butter cream so sweet it made his teeth ache. The waitress incident hadn't done much to lift the black mood. He could feel it tightening his jaw; Mouse was giving him the silent treatment. It hadn't been like this in his head. When he'd invited her to do something normal he'd imagined easy conversation in a cosy diner, just the two of them. He hadn't really taken into account her situation. She focused entirely on her son, leaning in to brush the floppy hair from his eyes, listening to his chatter about school and telly programmes. He envied how they were with each other, communicating without words in the way families do: a nod, a lift of the shoulder, a look.

It reminded him he'd had all that, and he'd fucked it up.

Sipping his coffee, he said, 'Has it always been just you and him?' Mouse looked affronted and he rushed on: 'I just wondered . . . You're very tight, the two of you.'

Her eyebrows shot up. William sucked up the last of his drink through a straw, breaking the tension with a noise like a bathtub emptying.

'William! If you're finished you can go through and look in the shop.'

He didn't need telling twice. He jumped up, almost knocking over his empty glass and disappeared.

'I'm sorry. I didn't mean to upset you.'

She shrugged. 'He's a bit sensitive about the father issue. He's curious, and I can't always deal with it.'

'Oh aye. I'm sorry about . . . before. I didn't mean to get in a bad mood. It happens. It just happens.'

'Walt. Stop apologising.' She leaned closer, put her elbows on the table and smiled at him. She had a wide smile when she used it, one that made you feel good inside, warm. 'I phoned that number you gave me, the one for the MoD. You never told me you'd been medically discharged.'

'We all have things we don't want to talk about, don't we?'

They shared a moment of perfect understanding, and for the first time since he'd arrived in Edinburgh he felt a measure of peace. He broke the silence first.

'So tell me, who's the daddy?'

That made her laugh, as he knew it would.

'Oh God.' She heaved a sigh, jammed her fingers into the sides of her hair and stared at the table. 'We were students, and he freaked out when I told him I was pregnant. He wanted to run a mile, so I let him.'

'What were you studying?'

'Nursing. My mum was a nurse in Inverness, before she met my father. I kind of always wanted to be a nurse too. I remember she kept her old uniform and we used to try it on, Alys and me. We'd put on grown-up shoes and bandage up our dolls. The hat was all lacy . . . Alys snatched it off me once and tore it and Mum gave the whole lot to the charity shop.' She was looking out of the window. He watched the memories play out behind her eyes. 'Alys wasn't interested in anything, but Mum taught me how to make beds, you know, with hospital corners?'

He nodded. He knew about hospital beds.

'She used to say, "Fitted sheets and duvets – fiddlesticks!

It's lazy bed-making, like you don't care enough. You want a smooth sheet, Maura. Not a wrinkle in the sheet. Wrinkles cause redness, leading to bedsores. Skin is everything – you must keep it in tip-top condition. Look after a patient's skin and you're half way to winning the battle."' Mouse gave a little laugh. 'I never really knew what the battle was.'

'Skin keeps us together, lass,' he said. *Even when we're coming undone inside.*

'I suppose it does. I never thought of it like that.'

'When did she die?'

His bluntness shook her out of the past; she sat up straighter. 'Just before William was born.'

There wasn't much he could say to that. Sympathy was overused and pointless. Instead he said, 'You'd make a good nurse.'

She blushed. 'You don't even know me!'

'I just meant you'd look good in the uniform.'

This time she laughed out loud, and the old lady at the next table looked up and smiled. She was starting to get him; that was progress.

'I'd better go and see what William is up to,' she sighed. 'He'll have spent all his pocket money on Victorian thimbles or something!' She started to get up and paused. 'You know, he goes round the house searching for things, like kids do at Christmas – prying into cupboards and drawers, going where he shouldn't go. And now he's checking up on my Facebook page! I sometimes think he's looking for evidence of who he is. Like he wants to fill in the gaps, the things I can't tell him.' She shook her head. 'Anyway, I'll see you in a minute.'

Walt drained his coffee, suddenly thoughtful. He felt for the button in his pocket. Rain was beginning to collect on the window, and he sat for a few minutes, watching the passers-by trudging along, bundled up in coats and hats. Eventually, he got up from the table and wandered across the lobby to the flea market. Edging past a middle-aged guy in black biker leathers who was sorting through a box of vinyl LPs, Walt spotted William and his mother at the far end of the shop. On impulse, Walt flipped the button from his pocket and approached the counter, where Mr Flea 'n' Tea was leafing through an old theatre programme. He looked up when Walt approached.

'Can you identify this?'

The guy didn't really fit the shop. He had the look of the outdoors about him, slightly weathered, with a sturdy physique. His hair was strangely brassy, like the wedding ring on his third finger; both looked fake. Walt offered the button on his palm, like a sugar cube, and the man gazed at it. 'I don't buy one-offs any more. If you had a set I might . . .'

'I'm not selling,' said Walt. 'I just want to know what it is. Quickly.' He was conscious that the kid could appear at any moment and that he had, in effect, stolen the thing. He still didn't know why he was being so secretive about it. The man was raking behind the till for a pair of cheap reading glasses. He put them on and held the button up to the light.

'Mmm.' He checked the reverse. 'I see.'

'What?' Walt could feel irritation storming in from somewhere. 'What is it?'

'That's the Imperial Eagle. German. World War Two. Probably from a tunic or a greatcoat. You don't have the greatcoat?'

'No, I don't.'

'Pity. I would have taken that off you. Very collectible. Nazi memorabilia is very sellable just now.'

Walt took the button back. Mouse was on her phone and she didn't look very happy. 'Okay, thanks, mate. Just wondered.'

Mouse was coming towards him, towing William along behind her. 'Walt! We have to go.'

'What's wrong?'

She was clearly distressed. 'Mrs Petrauska just called. Alys is sitting on the pavement crying.'

17

Alys was sitting on the pavement with her back to the railings, hugging her knees. Her hair hung forward and he couldn't see much of her face, but the sobs were raw and hoarse, like she'd been at it for a while. Mrs Petrauska was standing guard. Her face bore two camouflage streaks of mascara, and her palms were pressed together as if she was thinking about praying. Her relief at seeing back-up was explosive. She started gabbling, seizing Walt's arm as Mouse went into some kind of smooth choreography, handing the key to William and scooping an arm around her sister's heaving shoulders. It all looked too well rehearsed.

'This the second time this month, Maura!' Mrs Petrauska said. 'That poor girl, she need the *gydytojas*!'

'Doctor,' William translated. He'd developed a sudden air of confidence, racing up the steps, flashing the keys, swinging open the big heavy door.

Mouse was thanking Mrs Petrauska, bundling Alys towards the house. 'She hasn't been sleeping.'

'But you must get help!'

Walt detached himself, patted the woman's shoulder. 'We will. Thank you. Good night.'

And then they were in the hall and he was closing the door, with a last glance at Mrs Petrauska's mascara stains, like the shadows of the basement railings.

Alys had stopped sobbing. Her voice was now a nasally whine. 'You weren't there. You left me to do it all by myself.'

Mouse was looking at him pointedly. He realised the remarks were aimed at him. He stood with his back to the closed door and lifted his hand to his chest in an exaggerated gesture. 'Me?'

'I needed you, Walt!' The sobbing started again.

Walt hated women crying. He'd grown up around boys; when tears cropped up it was for a good reason – a fist fight, someone giving you a wedgie or stealing your new bike – and always the result of anger or frustration. As men the tears were quiet, hidden. Female tears were deeper, darker.

He appealed to Mouse. 'She said she wanted to be alone, to get on with her stuff!'

'When was this?' Mouse hugged Alys to her, smoothed her hair.

'Wednesday or Thursday, I guess. That's why I suggested we go out this morning. I've been bored off me tits for days. I can't stand having nothing to do, I . . .'

But Mouse wasn't listening. 'When did you last sleep, Alys? Have you eaten anything?'

Alys pulled away from her and staggered up the hall. 'I can't! It's all going wrong. I had this vision in my head but I can't make it work!' The backside of her jeans and her white sweater were snagged with the outside: dust and twigs and tiny leaves.

Mouse was biting her lower lip, the way William did. 'You can't work without any sleep. You're burned out, Alys. You need to go to bed.'

'I *can't* sleep, you idiot! You don't understand. The ideas won't let go of me! They're in my head *all* the time . . .' There began a fresh storm of weeping. Alys collapsed against the great polar bear, dissolving into his yellowy fur. William peered out from behind the kitchen door.

'Why don't you just go and have a little lie down.' Mouse followed Alys and took her by the thin shoulders. 'Come on. I'll change your pillowcases, that always helps you sleep. I'll sprinkle lavender oil on them, like Mum used to do. And I'll bring you up some hot milk.'

'No, no, no! The birds are all out! The birds are all out and I need to sort them!' She flung Mouse off violently. There was a noise like a slap, but Walt was guiding William back into the kitchen and didn't see what had happened. He could hear Mouse repeating her sister's words: 'The birds are all out? The birds are all *out*?'

'They are. Look.' The kid was pulling at Walt's sleeve. 'Look.'

'Shit.'

Alys kept all her roadkill in an upright freezer in the back corner of the kitchen. She'd given him the guided tour early on, explaining her filing system, demonstrating how each plastic drawer held different creatures: birds in the top, then rodents, then small furries such as rabbits and guinea pigs (maybe even kittens). Each specimen was bagged and tagged, her own personal morgue. Walt had felt physically sick. Now, the door of the freezer was standing open.

'Christ, is it empty? It is. It's empty. How much stuff did she have in here?' He crossed the room in a few strides and checked all the drawers.

Mouse spoke, right behind him. She sounded weary. 'It's always full, because people keep handing stuff in, like we're a bloody charity shop or something. She can't have stuffed them all. How big is this thing she's working on?'

Walt slammed the freezer door and turned around. 'Coffin-sized.'

'Oh God. I'll get her settled. You go down to the basement, Walt. See what she's done. William, get yourself some supper.'

'Can I have biscuits?'

'Yes.'

'Chocolate ones?'

'William!'

Walt made the short downward spiral to the basement. It meant going outside, of course, and it was still raining. It was a bad design flaw, not including an inside staircase. He tried to make the two-minute journey last, filling his lungs with fresh air, like a prisoner waiting for the cell door to clang shut. His heart was already racing, anticipating the dark.

It was the weeping, Mrs Petrauska's mascara stripes, the violence of Alys's reactions. It could all be superimposed on some other time, some other land. His base instincts refused to give up on him. *Re-experiencing is the most typical symptom of PTSD. This is when a person involuntarily and vividly relives the traumatic event in the form of flashbacks, nightmares or repetitive and distressing images or sensations. This can even include physical sensations such as pain, sweating and trembling.* NHS website, memorised.

The stench hit him when he opened the door. The little shop was clogged with it. Glassy eyes looked on in horror as he went behind the till and brushed aside the curtain. The only light was from the huge display case; it fanned out across the slate floor, interrupted by a hundred little speed bumps.

A hundred little bird corpses, laid out in neat rows like herring on a dock, and smelling just as bad. Defrosted, they were beginning to rot, tiny pools of liquid congealing under each one.

He started to shake. It began in his knees and travelled upwards, grabbing his guts. He was still rooted to the spot when Mouse came in.

'Oh my God.' She pressed the back of her hand to her nose. 'They must have been defrosting for days. Some of them are half rotten when we get them. What do we do? Can you refreeze them?' When he didn't speak she nudged his arm. 'Walt? It's not like meat, is it? Maybe we can refreeze them? Walt, what's wrong?'

'I need to get out of here.' His voice came out weird, strangled.

'You can't leave me with this! Look.' She seemed to sense his panic, hauled over a stool and pushed him down onto it. 'Breathe slowly. You look like you've seen a ghost . . .' She bit her lip and swung her gaze back to the corpses. 'Actually, I can sort this out myself. I've seen it all before. Why don't you go up and–'

'No. I'm okay.' He shook his head. 'I'm fine. You get a black bag. The best thing we can do is just sweep 'em up and put them in the bin. I'll get the dustpan.'

Mouse flipped on the main light. The place flooded with an awful certainty. All those fragile victims, concave under cold feathers and stiff claws. There was something horrifying about the way they were arranged in those neat rows. It was like the aftermath of an execution.

Not knowing where to start, Walt set to with the brush.

'Wait!' Mouse grabbed his arm. 'Which one's the wren?'

He glared at her. 'You're winding me up. You want me to check every one to find a fuckin' wren?'

'It's what she was working on. If we chuck them out, she'll go mental.'

They stood looking at the mess, trying not to breathe in the stink. Mouse's eyelashes were wet.

'Honestly,' she whispered, 'if she comes down and finds them all gone, she'll trash the place. You have no idea what it's like.'

Walt put down the brush. He wanted to loop his arm around her, offer a bit of comfort, but he was afraid she might take it the wrong way, so he just said, 'I do, bonny lass. I know what it's like.'

Mouse nodded. 'Oh God, we'll just have to dump them. Can't stand that smell.'

They worked in silence, Mouse holding the bag and Walt scooping up the corpses. He took the bag and knotted it. Mouse told him to stick it in the bin, but to make sure it was the right bin and not Mrs Petrauska's. The thought of Mrs Petrauska's reaction to finding dozens of rotting birds didn't bear thinking about. Walt found a red baseball cap lying on top of the bins. Was it William's? He held it up. It was grubby, well worn, with a peak that had once been white underneath but was now mushroom-coloured. He didn't think Mouse would let the boy wear such a thing, but he decided to take it with him, just in case. As he was about to walk away, a glimmer of something caught his eye. The funny little window, the one he'd noticed the time he'd come out to inspect the pipework, was ominously dark, and yet . . . He could have sworn he'd seen movement, or the ghost of a movement, like the flitting of a moth across a beam of light. He peered closer, but the grimy square remained stubbornly blank. Imagination plays tricks on you all the time; he knew that first-hand. Still . . . Whirling the dirty red cap around his index finger, he walked uncertainly back to the house.

18

In the kitchen, Mouse was hugging the kid. Smothered in her jumper, he was standing patiently, one eye visible between his fringe and her sleeve.

'The birds are gone,' Walt announced. 'Extinct.'

She didn't get the joke. 'You definitely put them in our bin?'

'I put them in the one marked "Dance Studio".'

'What?' She swung around, realised he was trying to lighten the mood and rolled her eyes. William escaped. 'Where are you going?'

'Just up to my room,' he said.

'Don't go near Auntie Alys's room. She needs to rest.'

'Here, kid. Is this yours?' Walt held up the cap by its grubby peak.

'It is not,' Mouse said straight away. 'Look at the state of it!'

William gazed at it with interest, but knew better than to touch it. 'I could keep it though. For my collection.'

'No!' Mouse glared at Walt. 'You should have put that in the bin too.'

Walt shrugged and hooked the offending article onto the back of a chair. As William scurried off, Walt went over to wash his hands at the sink.

'Is she sleeping?' He turned on the tap and scrubbed his hands with liquid soap.

Mouse folded her now-empty arms and hugged herself. 'No. She's lying quietly though, staring at the ceiling.'

'Should I go up?'

'Why should you?' She looked at him sharply.

He shrugged. 'Because she's my boss? I feel responsible.'

'Don't.'

'You heard what she said to me. I shouldn't have left her.'

'You don't need to feel responsible, and Walt . . .' She looked him full in the face, sternly, as if she were scolding William. 'Don't get too close to her.'

'I wasn't. I'm not.'

'Good. Alys is very vulnerable. She may look all flirty and confident, but underneath, she's her own worst enemy.'

'I get the picture.' He dried his hands slowly on a towel. He had the picture in his head: Alys giving him the come-on, touching her mouth to his. Maybe he'd been on his own too long. Mouse was eyeing him as if she'd just found a stash of porn under his bed. Turning away, she started rummaging through the cupboard under the sink, pulling out cloths and rubber gloves and bleach. He felt dismissed but something made him linger, a strong sense of injustice. He'd drifted in here for his own reasons. The job had suited him, and the room. He could go to ground for a while, living with these two strange, distant sisters, each with their own stuff going on and not much caring what he did or didn't do. Not asking about his past.

But he was getting pissed off with the way they only gave away so much, though the irony was not lost on him. He was *living* with them – surely he was entitled to more than a few crumbs of information?

Mouse flushed hot water into a basin. Steam surrounded her like mist as she snapped on yellow Marigolds. He wasn't going to let her blot away what had just happened like an inconvenient stain.

'So what's Alys's problem then? Bipolar? Autism? What?'

Mouse hefted the basin from the sink and made for the freezer, slopping water in her hurry to avoid the question. He followed her.

'If I'm working with her I need to know.'

'I don't know what it is.' She kneeled down and opened up the freezer drawers, releasing a faint whiff of death. 'She's always been like that. I suppose she's on the spectrum, somewhere. When she was little she was just a handful, like most kids. She was wilful, disruptive.' She sat back on her heels, pushing aside her hair with one clumsy yellow rubber hand. 'She was always in trouble at school, for breaking things and fighting.'

Walt came to stand right behind her. 'Maybe it's that attention deficit thing.'

'Don't know. Mum might have had her assessed, but Dad was a bit old-school. He didn't want people coming around prying, so it just got left, like a lot of other things.'

He couldn't see her face but the bitterness was unmistakeable.

'So is that why you stick around? To look after her?'

'Can you imagine how she'd cope on her own?' He could hear the threat of tears in her voice. The sound hurt him, and he reached round and pulled her up by the elbows and folded her into his arms. She stood there, not moving, like William had done, trying not to touch him with the wet rubber gloves. He moved back to look into her face, but she wouldn't catch his eye. She looked miserable, wet cheeks, red nose.

'You know what? I'm going to do what all good Brits do in a crisis.' He moved her firmly to the table and made her sit down. She pulled off the gloves with an air of defeat. Walt went over to the worktop and switched on the kettle. 'I've made tea all over the globe and I have a theory.' He'd got her interest, albeit reluctantly. 'All families have a tea triangle.'

'A tea triangle?' She looked at him like he was trying to sell her snake oil.

He demonstrated obligingly. 'Look, kettle here. Along the worktop, mug rack. And above the kettle . . .' He flung open a cupboard. 'Teabags. I rest my case.'

'It's an isosceles.' She perked up a bit, resting her chin in her hands.

'Correct. Now my mother favours the obtuse triangle. Kettle here, teabags here, near the sink, and mugs overhead in *this* cupboard.' He flipped open a different door.

Mouse shook her head. 'Yeah, but what about the sugar? And the milk?'

'Ee, now you're just making it complicated, like.'

She flashed her wide grin. 'All this proves is that you've spent far too much time drinking tea.'

'True. Unless . . .' He opened the fridge with a flourish. 'There is alcohol to hand. I see wine. Fancy a glass?'

She sat up straight, batted the idea away with a hand. 'No way. I've a kid upstairs and a sister who . . . No, I can't. Just make tea.'

'So you have a packed Saturday night, do you?'

'No, not exactly.'

'You'll be sitting watching *The X Factor* like everybody else. Have one glass.'

She sighed. 'Just one. A small one.'

'I'll stick on this pizza, to soak it up.' He laughed at her scowl. He didn't know why he was suddenly in a good mood, not with the way the last couple of hours had gone. He ripped open the pizza box and switched on the oven. The wine was a dry white, nice and chilled. He found two glasses and poured. The anticipation warmed him.

'So Alys was the wild one . . . when you were bairns?'

Mouse smiled. 'We were both wild. We lived in a castle, back then, so we had plenty room to be wild.'

'A castle? I'm impressed.'

'Don't be. It was a dump. Crumbling about our ears. Mum hated it but it had been in Dad's family for ages and I don't think he saw what she saw – the damp and the mice and the endless cleaning. We didn't see it either, as wee ones. We just enjoyed the space.'

'So tell me about it. I've never met anyone who lived in a

castle before.' He sat down and took a sip of his wine. She coloured a little, flattered by the attention.

'Oh God. There were draughts and leaks and it was dark everywhere, and most times when you put the light on, the bulbs would blow. Dad said it was the damp and the old wiring. Alys said it was the ghosts sucking up all the energy. She has a great imagination. I suppose my favourite place was down by the old cow byre that Dad used as a garage. I used to hide there, in amongst the weeds. I can still smell the crushed nettles and dock leaves . . . I loved the foxgloves. You could make the little purple bells pop if you squeezed them the right way, or you could wear them on your fingers like fairy thimbles.'

She looked suddenly very young. 'I remember my mother pegging sheets out on the rope. She'd prop it up with a forked pole, and the laundry used to dance in the wind.'

Her eyes sparkled when she looked at him, but there must have been something in his face – she stopped and raised the glass to her lips, taking a cautious sip. 'Sorry. I'm being boring.'

'No, no. I was just thinking of my mother's washing line.'

'Not your mother?' she teased.

'Nope. Just the washing line.' He drained his glass in one gulp and got to his feet. The chair scraped harshly on the floor. 'I'll check on the pizza.'

19

Mam's washing line is wrapped so tight around a limb of the old tree that the rope has rubbed a gall in the bark. Robert isn't that good on trees; not like Steven who can name trees, garden birds and movie stars like he's eaten an encyclopaedia. The tree smells like the green disinfectant Mam puts down the bog and its bark . . . He loves its bark. It's thick and scabby, like a pine cone, with deep cracks you can stick your fingertips in. Sometimes it flakes away and the wood beneath is all smooth and dewy like new skin.

They're all up in the tree: Robert and Steven and Tom, perched in the lower branches like cats. Tom's a ginger tom, but you can't say that or he'll clout you. They've been watching a Western; the villain had been hoisted into a tree and hanged, his dusty spurred boots jerking in mid-air. Mam had come in and turned off the telly and they'd all groaned, and she'd snapped, 'Get outside and play. Watching all that rubbish.'

So they'd fled to the back garden. Sitting up in the tree with legs wrapped around branches they eye the washing line and wonder what hanging is like. Robert is worried about how tight the rope is around the branch.

'It's making it bleed, look.'

'That's sap.' Steven peers at the wound over his glasses. 'Tree blood.'

'I think we should untie it.'

'Mam'd kill you,' says Steven, screwing up his nose.

'Do you bleed when they hang you?'

'Man, Robert!' Tom groans as if everyone knows the answer to that. 'You ask the dumbest things!'

'You don't bleed but you pee yourself,' Steven replies gravely.

'Oh, gross!' There's general fidgeting at the grossness of it.

Tom eyes Steven suspiciously. 'They don't show that on the films.'

'Our mam turned it off before the peeing part.'

'We're going to see *The Goonies* tonight,' says Steven, changing the subject. 'Wanna come?'

'Awesome! I'll ask me da.' Tom slithers down from the tree and the others flex their elbows.

'I'm fed up out here,' Steven huffs. 'This tree don't do anything. I'm away in to play wi' me *Star Wars* stuff.' He hops down too, leaving Robert alone, lodged in a bum-bruising 'V' between the branches.

It is so quiet without the others; it's like listening to the inside of a big seashell. He can hear tiny things: the shivering of the leaves, a hornet buzzing, the far-off bleating of a sheep. He presses his cheek against the rough bark and pretends to be Invisible Tree Man. He plays this game often, imagining his skin turning the colour of compost and the tree soaking him up until he is part of it, invisible, so well hidden that Mam will never find him at bedtime. He could stay out all night in the velvety midnight and take down the rope so the tree stops bleeding. Though Mam would be sure to find him at some point and if it meant she'd had to leave *Coronation Street* to come out after him in her slippers she'd throw a huge wobbler and they'd be in the bad books for days. Reluctantly, he peels himself away from the bark and jumps to the ground.

20

He'd gone to bed about nine, only because Mouse had made it plain she wouldn't sit downstairs arsing booze with him. Once William had come down to get his share of the pizza she'd determinedly washed up and wiped the surfaces down with something strong and lemony, leaving him feeling about as welcome as a ketchup smear. Fuck, did she ever stop cleaning? What was she trying to wash away? He'd retreated upstairs, taking the remainder of the bottle with him, but not the glass. She'd already washed it. He took off his things and lay on the bed in his T-shirt and boxers, necking wine from the bottle and wishing there was a telly in his room, or music, or anything that didn't require him to think.

He must have finished the bottle and drifted off with the light on, because one minute he was contemplating the shiny walnut wardrobe and the next he woke with a sick start, not knowing, in the way that you do, whether this was a dream or real. Corpses in neat regimental rows, like birds. They didn't die like that. They died untidily, with parts missing. Sometimes he could still see the parts, coated in sand, dangling from trees. He never saw his own foot, but he dreamed about it often.

He was suddenly aware he was being watched and every hair stood up on his body, every nerve stretched. He reached for his gun but found only the duvet bunched beneath his fists. By the time he'd realised it was William, his breathing was coming in shallow gasps and his heart was hammering in his ears.

'For fuck's sake! What the hell are you doing?'

William's blue eyes widened. They were fixed on his legs, or at least on the space where his right foot should be. He'd taken off his prosthesis when he lay down.

'Mum wouldn't want you saying the F-word in front of me.' The boy wandered to the end of the bed.

Walt lay there like a landed fish, still trapped in his own panic. 'She wouldn't want you coming into a strange man's bedroom either. You shouldn't be here.'

'You're not strange.' The kid peered at his stump and asked the obvious. 'What happened to your leg?'

'IED blast. I was one of the lucky ones. And it was just my foot. That was lucky too.'

'You've still got your knee.' William looked solemnly at his stump, like a doctor. All he needed was the white coat and a pen to point out the damage to his students. He was close, head bent to examine the scar.

Walt sighed, lay back again and covered his eyes with his forearm, waiting for the questions.

'Does it hurt?'

'Not so much now.'

'It looks like you never had a leg there, the skin is healed up so good.'

'Yeah?' Walt lowered his arm. He'd stopped obsessing about the stump. It was there, deal with it. The physio had been tough, but it was something to pit himself against, and the lads in the centre . . . most had been worse off. The damage was colossal, but the comradeship, the black humour, had kept him going. It was only when he got home, when he realised he was on his own, that the hurting began.

'It's kind of all stitched up neat like you never had a leg. Skin's amazing.'

Walt swallowed, half smiling at the ceiling. A tear had gathered in the corner of his eye and it slid a wet trail down his cheek to the pillow. 'Skin hides a lot,' he whispered.

'I'd better go back to bed. I thought I heard a noise. Did you hear it?'

Walt propped himself up on his elbow to check his watch on the bedside table. 'What time is it? Jesus, it's nearly midnight. What are you doing out of your scratcher?' He registered that the kid was in his pyjamas, his hair sleep-ruffled.

'I just told you – I heard a noise.'

'Probably your mad auntie stuffing kittens.' He rolled over to the side of the bed, sat up and rubbed his eyes. 'Forget that. I shouldn't have said that. Go on up to bed.'

William stood there, dumbly.

'Scoot.' Walt made walking movements with his fingers.

'I'm scared.'

'Eh?'

'I heard something. What if there's someone in the house?'

'There's no one in the house, kid. I sleep like a tripwire, I would have heard them. Want me to take you upstairs?'

William nodded fiercely.

The attic staircase was a scaled-down, flimsier version of the main one. Though it began on the landing outside his own bedroom door, Walt had never had call to venture up there until now.

Walt sighed. He suspected this might be a ploy so the lad could witness the fitting of the prosthesis, something to tell his classmates. *We've got this guy staying and his leg got blown off and I've seen the stump and everything.*

He strapped himself into the false leg. William was fascinated.

'State of the art titanium that.' Walt gave it a slap. 'Fifteen thousand quid's worth. Only the best for Her Maj's troops.'

'Wouldn't it be cheaper if they sent you somewhere where there's no bombs?'

There was no answer to that. Walt got to his feet. 'Look, kid. See my coat over there, on the chair? Go in the pocket and there's something there of yours. You left it behind when you were going through your stuff.'

William dived on the coat, rifled through the pockets and held the button aloft.

'Wow! Can I keep it? It's awesome!'

Walt chuckled. Should he put on his jeans? Mouse would have a fit if she saw the two of them parading around the house and him in his boxers. 'It's yours anyway, you clown!'

'It's not mine.'

'But it was on the chair, in the sitting room.'

William shrugged. 'Definitely not mine. I know my collection.'

Walt seized the button. The Imperial Eagle winked at him in the light.

21

He went on his third tour without Tom.

The place was hotter, dustier and tenser than he remembered. Home seemed further away and the jokes were blacker than they'd ever been before. Into the gaping Tom-shaped hole wandered Scoff. The mongrel was the same shade as the desert, and in those first days, when he lay down in the shade, his ribs were sharp as coat hangers, his flanks concave. Half of one floppy ear had been torn off, his fox's nose was tattooed with bite marks, and when Walt picked him up to take him to the vet, he peed himself in fear.

The Afghanis had no love for dogs; dogs were unclean. The Taliban had banned dog fighting but the ban was seldom enforced. All the most powerful local officials were said to be involved in it. Out on foot patrol, Walt would see the big barrel-chested Kuchis, the native breed, growling at the end of their chains: a warrior dog for a warrior people. The matches were staged mainly in the winter months, when the dogs were more energetic and their wounds healed faster. It was about money and respect. But most of all, money. Even in the tiny villages, with the men crouched in a circle and the dogs locked together in battle, the stakes were high: money, cars, reputations. A village elder had told him once that the dogs were fed on sheep's feet and eggs to build them up and make them aggressive, while in the same tent sat three tiny children, thin as sparrows.

The dogs that lost were turned out to fend for themselves. He couldn't work out which was the better option.

In a land of no pets, Scoff, as the lads dubbed him, quickly figured out how to be one. He chose Walt's bunk to sleep on, stretching out like an electric blanket, and waited for him coming off patrol, eyes like chocolate, tail whipping up the dust. Every ten minutes spent with Scoff was ten minutes of not being on the front line. He felt his heart scab over one lick at a time.

Scoff took to going on routine patrols with the unit, riding in the Mastiff like he'd been born to it, his tongue lolling and eyes shining. The day it happened, there'd been a heavy fog. They didn't leave base until 1000 hours, sharing the usual banter as they got their kit together. They stopped not long after to do a vulnerable point check, assessing the threat of IEDS. Walt jumped out with his second in command; he went to the right, Mac to the left. The place, usually bustling with market traders and livestock, was quiet. Something cold fingered the back of Walt's neck. He walked carefully around the piles of rubble and garbage that littered the road, his hands sweating on his rifle. Something didn't feel right. He turned to Mac.

He may have got the words out before the bomb detonated, but he wasn't sure. He was still trying to speak when the others rushed to his side. Someone was doing something with a tourniquet. 'You're all right, mate,' said Mac, 'you've still got your crown jewels.' He wasn't in pain, not then, but he could feel something warm under his leg. His eyes were full of dust. It was much later, when they flew him back to England, that he found out Scoff had jumped out of the Mastiff after him and taken the full force of the blast.

22

Alys slept all the next day. Walt looked in on her once; she was curled up under the white cotton duvet like a princess. Her skin was waxy, lips parted as she breathed softly through her mouth. Mouse must have been in there: everything was neat, ordered in a way that Alys could never have achieved. Her clothes – the bloodstained sweater and skinny jeans – had been laundered and folded and placed on a chair. The long brown boots she always wore stood to attention, heels together, at the end of the bed. He could imagine Mouse pottering around in here, taking control because she could, with her sister sleeping like a baby. She could clean and tidy and make it all okay.

With Alys wounded in action, it fell to Walt to man the fort. He was never keen to be alone in the basement, but there was a delivery to be put away. He'd placed the order himself, according to Alys's instructions: tow and raffia for stuffing and fixing, preservative and artificial bird feet, almost as cutting-edge as his own. 'Suitable for jays and magpies', the online description had said. Opening the studio door and flicking the light switch, he found himself daydreaming about rows of prosthetic human feet in some secret warehouse. Maybe they'd have labels attached to their big toes: 'Suitable for lesser-spotted, dark-haired Aquarian.' The idea made him chuckle.

He'd left the boxes behind the till, and he was already rooting in the drawer for a Stanley blade when he realised the floor was clear. He was sure he'd left them there: six cardboard boxes.

Still gripping the knife he went through into the workshop, automatically sniffing the air. The whiff of dead bird had faded, but it had been replaced by something else: a sort of school-dinner-hall fustiness. The skin on the back of his neck crawled and his grip tightened on the knife. He remembered the boxes. How could six boxes disappear? Would Alys have moved them? She certainly wouldn't have emptied them and put them away. Then he noticed the pink invoice, flattened out on Alys's workbench and weighted down by a small pair of scissors. He scouted round the room, bent to look beneath the workbench. There they were. He counted to make sure: six boxes. He straightened up. Had Alys risen from her bed and moved them? It hardly seemed likely. He was suddenly afraid to touch anything. He needed to get up to the surface, to remain in the light.

Brain fizzing with the possibilities, he ended up in the kitchen, mechanically raiding the fridge. There were a few cans of beer left; he'd bought a load in specially, much to Mouse's disgust. Snagging them by the plastic tag, he slammed the door shut. It was only as he was passing the table that he smelled the coffee. Alys's place setting was, as usual, untouched, but the mug, her special mug, was filled with coffee.

His breathing went funny, became lodged high up in his throat. Alys *hated* coffee. She liked tea, milky, with two sugars. Baby tea, William called it; even he didn't drink tea that weak. So who was drinking black coffee from Alys's mug? He dipped in his pinkie. The liquid was stone cold, as if it had been hanging around for hours; a pre-dawn caffeine fix.

With the beers banging against his thigh, Walt exited the kitchen. Had Alys had another episode? Had she been up in the small hours, consumed by a mad notion for strong coffee? He dropped the beers at Shackleton's feet and jogged up the stairs. Her bedroom door was slightly ajar, and he paused to catch his breath. He always experienced this sick lurch of the stomach before entering

Alys's vicinity. It was disturbing. He saw himself in her damaged eyes, and he knew he would leave here the worse for it. He'd brought back all sorts of shite from Afghanistan, stuff you couldn't pack in your kit bag, and he didn't have room for any more.

He pushed open the door. Alys was still out for the count. He couldn't imagine she'd had a mad midnight coffee break after moving six boxes of taxidermy supplies.

Creeping back downstairs, he collected his beer and shut himself in the cold green sitting room. There was rugby on TV. Mouse had taken William to the cinema, and the house was too quiet. He'd grown used to the sound of William jumping down the stairs two at a time, speaking to the great polar bear or the cats. Mouse sang along to the radio in the kitchen, when she thought no one was about. She liked Ed Sheeran, knew all the words. He wanted to ask her about the coffee (Mouse would *never* have used Alys's mug) and the boxes, to share this anomaly with her. He missed her, and the realisation hit him hard, like a punch to the abs.

He turned up the commentary and tried not to think.

Later, he went down to the basement again. He'd look at the date on the invoice; maybe it was an old one that hadn't been filed. He felt like a kid, scrabbling to slam on the lights before the bogeyman got there. The trouble was, he realised, the bogeyman had been there before him.

A sharp stink of something wild and musky alerted him to trouble. There was a dead fox lying on top of the glass display case in Alys's workroom. It was stretched out and moth-eaten, like a vintage stole. The little birds underneath looked haunted and trapped.

He couldn't see the fox's face. There was no way of knowing whether it was stuffed or simply deceased. The only thought that invaded his head was that it didn't walk there by itself. Someone had brought it in.

He went as close as he dared, trying to block out the smell. If he was looking for clues he could find only one. The red baseball cap was now on the workbench beside the invoice.

23

When he went down to the basement on Monday morning, Alys was already there, looking composed and freshly showered; even just standing in the doorway, he got the scent of peach. Her hair was damp, scooped up into a neat knot. Perched on a stool, she was leaning into the display case, adjusting a fine detail of moss with a pair of tweezers. She was bathed in a warm glow from the solitary lamp, but there was something else about her, a sort of suppressed fizz, like she was lit from inside.

He'd made no sound, but she glanced around anyway. Her skin was still pale, washed out in the bright light, but her eyes were clear. It was impossible to read her mood, to know what to say for the best. He had never mentioned to Mouse about the coffee, the fox, the red cap, the unexplained delivery. There had to be a rational explanation.

'Sorry we had to dump the birds,' he said. That sounded lame, and even a bit brutal.

She shrugged. 'I have a contact in the country. He's going to bring me some more birds. A wren too!'

'Is that the contact who brought you the dead fox?' She didn't answer. 'Does he have a key?'

She looked more like her old self, although he wasn't too sure, now, of the real Alys. He didn't know her well enough, and anyway, that's what happens when your mind starts playing up. You lose sight of who you are and so does everyone else. Even the people who know you best, who love you, don't know how to be around you any more.

How did someone fulfil a large order for birds? He shied away from the thought.

Ignoring his questions completely, she said, 'So in the meantime, I've sketched out what's in my head. So I don't lose it.'

Lose the idea? Or the plot? She fished a large piece of cartridge paper from under the table and held it out to him. He moved closer to take it from her. She was talented. The whole tableau, the vision that made her go crazy, was set out in detail worthy of a Leonardo sketch. In frozen, wintry colours she had captured a band of birds: a crow in a periwig, starlings in neckerchiefs and blackbirds with muskets; sparrows, goldfinches, even a robin in a Dick Turpin hat. And in the centre, the wren, lolling dramatically from Moodie's gibbet. *To be hanged by the neck until you are dead*. No mercy.

Walt thrust the page back at her, and if she noticed anything she didn't let on. Instead, she flashed her lightning smile and said, 'I *love* starting on a project! Love it, I get so excited opening up a new specimen my hands shake!'

'Your hands shake?'

'Yes – just imagining the anatomy inside! The colours, the . . .'

He had to stop her. He put his hands on her, on her shoulders, felt his palms close over the bones. 'Don't, Alys. Jesus, you're weird.'

She was still smiling. Her teeth were very white, like she never chewed anything with colour in it. He imagined them biting into his skin. Her breathing was shallow; he could see it pushing at the little bones in her neck. Her arms grew warm under his palms. She was whispering something, her lips dry like bruised leaves; she slid off the stool, deliberately bumping into him, into his hips. He hadn't meant to be that close but, like the wren, he'd been too slow to move. She rubbed against him like a cat. Belly to belly. There was something wildly intimate about it: that they weren't even touching or kissing but she'd closed the gap between them just the same. He was shocked at his reaction; he felt the twitch of his erection and so did she, and she grinned all the more and this time closed the gap all the way, pressing against him and looping her arms about his neck. There was something greedy about the way she pressed her mouth to his. The scent of peaches was overwhelming. He knew he should push her away from him, but he felt like jelly. Or his knees did anyway; everything further north was rock hard.

She whispered, 'I want to ask you something,' and he replied, 'What, what do you want to ask?' and their voices intermingled like their breath.

'William told me about your leg.'

Kiss.

'Mm?'

She pulled back an inch, stroked his face. 'You never told me about your leg.'

'My foot. It's just my foot.' Like it really mattered – even though it did. He'd slept with a girl since it happened, just to affirm life, but he was afraid of the pity face, the sympathy. Alys kissed him again, hungrily; he could feel the shake in her and he was shaking too.

'I want to see it.'

'What?'

She leaned back, licked her lips. Really licked them, and that light in her eye ... He should have known Alys would be different.

'I want to see it – the scar, the stump. Show me.'

An icy chill shaved through his bones. Alys held his gaze. Her hand travelled to his waist, to his groin. Her touch burned through the denim of his jeans. Alys, who always avoided eye contact, was looking into him like he was empty, a vacant skin for her to probe, to play with.

'No.' He pulled away from her quick, clever fingers.

'Alys, have you seen the ...' Mouse suddenly appeared in the doorway. 'The phone bill.' Her voice dropped away. Walt pushed Alys to one side, kept his back turned, embarrassed. Alys was unfazed.

'Thought you were at work.'

'Obviously.'

'Don't give me that look, Mouse!'

Walt risked a glance at Mouse. Her mouth set in a tight line and she was blushing furiously, and he felt *himself* going red. Why the hell was he embarrassed? He was a free agent. Don't get involved, he told himself. Jesus, Mouse made him feel like a naughty schoolboy.

'It could have been William coming through this door!' Mouse snapped. 'It's not on.'

Walt had an inappropriate urge to laugh. The bulge in his jeans was subsiding, so he turned around and tried to reason with her.

'Sorry, Mouse. It wasn't what it looked like.' For some reason he wanted her to believe it was meaningless, but Alys was getting all uppity.

'Sorry? Don't apologise! This is my house. Mouse, if you don't like it, you know what to do.' She flounced back to the display case.

Mouse stormed out.

Walt dithered between them. 'Why did you say that?'

She didn't answer. On impulse he followed Mouse back to the house and caught up with her in the hallway. She stood in the shadow of Shackleton and turned on him, eyes spitting fire.

'When did my son see your leg?'

He'd been rehearsing what to say about Alys – *I was fighting her off, honest* – but he wasn't expecting that.

'Um, couple of nights ago, I think. He came into my room.'

'Into your room?' Her eyebrows disappeared into her hairline. Above her the polar bear looked down his lofty nose and snarled.

'He thought he heard something. It was late, I'd been sleeping . . . I took him back up to bed.'

'And he saw your leg.'

'He was curious. Look, let's stick to the problem.'

'You are the fucking problem!'

He flinched. Her hair was wild, her face in shadow. He didn't know this person any more. She was a cornered bear.

'We were fine until you rolled up,' she spat.

'You weren't fine!' he shouted back. 'You're trapped here playing nurse, cleaner and fuck knows what else to a woman who needs some kind of diagnosis. You're bringing up a child in a place where there are so many secrets he thinks he can uncover them by turning the place over like a cat burglar. All I did was switch on the light!'

He was breathing hard and so was she, like they'd been for a hard sprint together. Her eyes glittered like ice chips.

'Stay away from Alys,' she said.

'Oh, I intend to. You heard what she said about my leg?'

Mouse shook her head slowly.

'I thought she was going to ask for the blown-off foot so she could stuff it and add it to her little shop of horrors.'

'Don't.' Mouse slipped a hand across her stomach.

'Don't? If you distrust anyone around William, it should be her, not me.'

'That's a horrible thing to say!'

'Don't tell me it's not at the back of your mind every single day – *what is she going to do next?*'

The ice chips were melting. He didn't want to see her cry. He took himself off up the stairs, but he could feel her gaze on his back.

24

The next morning, Walt popped out for a fag break to find that someone had left a Tesco bag tied to the railings. Lighting up slowly, he gazed at it for several seconds, as if expecting it to move. Eventually, clamping the fag in his lips, he untied the handles. The bag was heavy, and he let it bump to the ground before peering in. A rabbit's dead face stared back at him. There was blood around the creature's nose; the delicate pink insides of its ears were mashed against the skull. He ground out the cigarette, retied the bag with shaking fingers, and carried it, at arm's length, into the kitchen. There seemed no other place for it than the bottom drawer of the freezer. He squashed it in, giving the door a hefty slam for good measure.

He lingered way too long in the kitchen, brewing coffee he didn't want, anything to avoid going back to the basement. When the doorbell rang it gave him a start. What now? Another loony with another carcass?

It was Mrs Petrauska. When he opened the door she was standing in some kind of ballet pose, bearing a dish wrapped in a checked tea towel.

Please don't let it be rabbit stew.

'Ah, Valter! I have for you *balandėliai*, a dish from my home in Lithuania. I make too much.'

She glided in as he was searching for a suitable reply. A quick stab of her feet on the welcome mat and she was heading straight for the kitchen. He followed in her wake, inhaling the scent of cabbage and onions and pepper, mixed with the sickly perfume she always wore. She placed the dish on the worktop as if she were laying a wreath, making a performance of it, backing away, poppy-painted fingers extended, and then the daintiest of pirouettes and she was facing him, eyes black as raisins.

'So tell me – how is she, Alys?'

'Um . . . fine, I think.'

'You know, Valter . . .' She came up close to him, placed a be-ringed hand upon his arm. The scent of roses wafted up from her bodice and he held his breath. 'This is not the first time she go like zis. Oh no.' She moved back, wagging her finger. 'At Christmas, I found her drunk in ze back garden with a man. They were outside my kitchen window, making noise, and when I say to her move on, she fly at me with a hammer! A hammer! I was going to call ze police, but Maura was so upset I could not.'

'Well, everyone can get drunk, Mrs P.' He wondered how long this was going to take. Though finding out about the hammer was a new twist.

'And the cats!'

'The what?'

'Cats! Breeding all over ze place. Apart from ze old white one, she past it. But all the other cats, they hanging around the bins, having kittens in my shed . . .'

'Kittens?'

'Breeding everywhere! I say to her you need to get zem snipped.'

'What happens to the kittens?'

'Who knows?' She made an extravagant gesture. 'Maybe the rats eat them! Zis is where I go now, to scrub ze bins. I came out yesterday and here is a rat, a dead one, lying on my bin and out comes ze Lady Alys and scoops 'im up. I say, "What you do wiz 'im? You crazy." And she jest smile and say, "I put 'im in an Elvis suit." An Elvis suit!'

'Jesus Christ. She's going to stuff it.' He ruffled his hair in agitation. The woman raised beetle-brows at his outburst.

'I told you.' Mrs Petrauska did the circling crazy sign again with her fingertip. 'Anyway, you enjoy my *balandėliai*. It is cabbage rolls, wiz pork. The name means "little doves". Enjoy!'

Little doves? They'd come to the wrong house. He suddenly didn't feel hungry.

The manic trilling of the phone made him jump; he grabbed a pen. Usually it was someone looking for Alys's more mundane services: a hunter with a trophy stag; the museum wanting her to patch up a walrus. Searching the kitchen worktop for a spent envelope, he thrust the receiver into the crook of his neck.

'Little Shop of Horrors,' he quipped. 'How can I help?'

'Walt, is that you?' Mouse's voice was all scratchy at the other end. Walt stopped rummaging, moving the receiver to his other ear. They'd done their best to avoid each other for almost a week, but the line crackled with unfinished business.

'Yeah, it's me. What's wrong?'

'I'm at the care home.'

Her voice dropped. Her dad was agitated. She couldn't leave. Their exchange was brief and stilted.

'William gets out of school at three.'

'I'll meet him.'

'I rang Mrs Petrauska but . . .'

'She's cleaning the bins.'

'She's what?'

'Rats.'

'Rats? Again? For heaven's sake. I wouldn't ask you but . . .'

'It's cool.'

'I'm stuck.'

Yeah, he thought, it stuck in her throat to ask him. He had her on the wrong foot and he kind of liked it. He was sick of dicking around; in the army you knew where you were, who you could trust and who trusted you. The lads always had your back, on patrol in Helmand or in a tough bar in the middle of Newcastle. It was unspoken. But he'd been cut loose from all that; lost his band of brothers and stumbled on the sisters from hell. Mouse hadn't trusted him from the start, never given him a chance. She didn't trust him around her child, around Alys, and it cut deep because a part of him knew she was right.

But she was *stuck*.

'Tell me where the school is.'

25

'We shouldn't have come here,' Walt said. 'Your mother won't like it.'

'She won't mind.' William's voice was muffled with toffee.

'Meet him at the newsagent's,' his mother had said. 'Not at the school gate because that's uncool. Meet him at the newsagent's but don't let him go in. He'll spend his money on crap and won't eat his tea.'

But William had pulled a fast one, darting into the shop before Walt could stop him.

The place was full of kids in grubby white shirts, boys mainly. Perhaps they needed more sugar than girls. What was that old rhyme? *Lads are made of slugs and snails and puppy dogs' tails*; he could see that in the wriggling of their wiry bodies, grimy hands counting coins. They were all yelling over each other, getting louder and louder until the shrillness drilled into his brain and he just wanted to get out. The Asian guy behind the counter was well used to it. He looked bored, twisting the lids off jars of jazzies, wine gums, gobstoppers. Chocolate buttons melting in sweaty paws. Walt felt like a heron in a swamp of minnows. He spied William and grabbed him by his green parka. The coat was way too warm for the mild weather, but his mother was afraid the wind might blow on him.

'Hey, kid, come on. I didn't sign up for this. Home. Now.'

'Hang on till I get some bootlaces.'

'Well, I'll be outside, mate. I cannot stand this.' He made for the door. It closed behind him with a dull *thwack*. He was standing on the pavement next to a billboard: 'TEACHERS IN PAY DISPUTE'. Christ, they deserved every penny.

The quiet was blissful after the shop. Even the cars sounded like they were rolling on sand. The door banged again and William was beside him, rummaging in a paper bag. The pencil-case smell of school wafted up from his hair.

'Want some?' William handed over a liquorice bootlace. It was a bit mangled, sticking to his palm. Walt had eaten worse. He shoved it in his mouth, enjoying the rubbery aniseed taste.

'Man, that takes me back. Me brother and me used to buy those with our pocket money at the garage.'

'Garage?'

'We were out in the country. It was a petrol station and shop. It had toilets too. The last bog before Scotland.'

'Really?' William looked impressed. 'So what if you didn't go on the way past? Where was the next bog?'

'Oh, Jedburgh, I guess. Yeah, I think there were bogs in Jedburgh.'

'Oh. How many brothers do you have?'

'One brother, Steven. I had a mate who was like a brother.'

William was staring at him with interest, cheeks working, lumpy with liquorice. 'What was his name?'

'Tom. He died.'

'Oh. What did he die of?'

'There was a bomb with his name on it. Look, kid, we'd better get home.' He turned to go, but William pulled at his sleeve.

'Let's go and see my granddad!'

'Your mother didn't say anything about that. I think we should just go . . .'

'No, let's! Pleeease. I haven't seen Granddad in ages. Mum won't mind.'

And so there they were, standing in the foyer of the home. It was the sort of great pile that had probably once belonged to a captain of commerce and his delicate daughters. You could imagine them ringing for the servants and taking tea in the parlour. The elaborate cornices and the grand staircase had survived, but everything else had been forced into a care-home shape: walls the colour of leek soup; carpets ripped up and replaced with something wipe-clean. Fire extinguishers, safety notices, wheelchair ramps. Someone had taken an angle grinder to the art nouveau tiles to accommodate the lift, leaving ugly scarred edges. Leaving your folks here, your father, would feel unnatural, a forced fit.

'We shouldn't have come here,' Walt said. 'Your mother won't like it.'

'She won't mind.'

A familiar figure trotted past with an armful of flowers. It was Mouse's friend with the geeky glasses. What was she called again? She pulled up short, purple tulip petals cascading to the floor.

'Hello! What are you two doing here?'

'How many jobs have you *got*?' Walt cut across her greeting, and she laughed and said it was just volunteering, a few hours every week, for her CV, and then she bowed down to William and said, 'Are you here to see your granddad? Why don't you go in? Your mum will be there soon, she's just in with the manager.'

'Okay.' William headed off and Walt's hand shot out and snagged him by the hood of his parka.

'Hold it, kid. We should wait for your mam.'

Fee – Walt suddenly remembered her name – waved them away. 'Go ahead, it's fine. Maura won't mind.'

Maura *will* mind. Walt wanted to say no, you needed permission to do things around Mouse, she's that kind of person, but he was taken up with the way Fee had called her Maura. He always thought of her as Mouse. All his mates had a handle of some kind – Mac, Chalky, Muddy (his last name was Waters) – but it occurred to him that Mouse's nickname was a dated family in-joke. He must remember to call her Maura in future.

Fee was telling William just what he wanted to hear: Granddad was watching telly in the day room. Yes, David Dickinson had been on when she'd last looked in. The kid took off like a whippet. Walt stalked after him.

The day room was the first door on the left. Everything about it was full on: the heating, the volume of the TV, the smell of piss. The screen was so enormous, Dickinson's face was stretched out of shape, bloated and brown. By contrast, the residents were as white as shed-grown mushrooms. They sat around the edges of the room in various stages of wilt, most sleeping, some with eyes fixed on the telly. One woman in a brown wig and a stained polyester cardigan strained forward with an empty smile, desperate for company.

Jesus. Walt wiped his face with his hand. *Jesus, Tom, at least you escaped this.* Death wasn't pretty, but waiting around for it was worse.

William was standing beside a man who wasn't even looking at him. The old boy was picking threads out of a ruined tartan rug, and judging by the holes in it, that was how he spent his days. His fingers were clawed, nails thick and yellow as toenails, engrained with something brown. All sense of recognition was gone: eyes empty, sunk into the bony hollows of his skull. He had three-day stubble, not just forgot-to-shave-this-morning stubble, but proper don't-give-a-fuck-stubble. Walt fingered his own chin, feeling the rasp of it. They hadn't washed him either. The nauseating sourness was inescapable.

William was still standing there, and when he said 'Granddad?' in a little voice and got zero reaction, Walt stepped in and squeezed his shoulder.

'William's come to see you, sir,' he said in the too-loud voice you always swear you'll never use with old folk. 'You remember William?'

He'd got his attention. The old boy glanced up. His mouth was gummy, like he needed a drink, but he managed to speak.

'Coby?'

'Um . . .' Walt looked at the boy, who shrugged. 'I'm *Walt*.' Still too loud. 'This is your grandson?'

'Coby?'

The carers bustled in behind them with a tea trolley. A blank-faced young girl came towards them, blue uniform straining over puppy fat, balancing a steaming cup and saucer.

'Is that for him? You can't give him that. He'll scald himself.'

'Are you a relative?' she asked. She had a baby face and round eyes ringed in black. She reminded him of a panda.

'He is,' he said, shoving William. The girl was manhandling a table with one hand, cup wobbling in the other. Walt caught hold of the table. 'If you're going to leave that tea there, don't.' His voice was dangerously low.

The girl's bubblegum lips tightened. 'Are you trying to tell me my job?'

'Are you telling me you know what you're doing?'

'What did you just say?'

'I said for a carer you're doing a shit job. This guy is filthy. He stinks of piss and he needs a shave. These old boys like to be smart, clean. They wear ties and bull their shoes. He needs to be *cared for*.'

The girl's lip quivered. 'I'm going to call my line manager now.'

'You do that, darlin'. Put some more milk in that tea and I'll help him drink it.'

She clunked the tea down on the table, slopping it into the saucer, and stormed off.

William was clapping. 'Aw, man, that was dead good, Walt!'

'Coby?' said the old man.

'Who's Coby? Have a sip of tea, sir.' Walt raised the cup to his lips. 'Take it easy now. It's a bit hot.'

'No, no, no.' The old man was getting agitated, fidgeting in his chair; his eyes suddenly lit up. 'Coby!' He knocked the cup flying, showering himself with hot tea; Walt and William jumped back as the cup smashed into white, institutional pieces at their feet.

'Walt!' Mouse's voice was as sharp-edged as the fragments of crockery. He glanced around to see the room full of people: Mouse, the sullen girl, Fee and a middle-aged woman with a fixed smile and Maggie Thatcher hair.

'Get a mop, Michaela,' the woman said through the smile. 'We haven't been introduced.' She proffered a hand to Walt, stepping over the spilled tea on clicking heels. 'This is a relative of yours, Maura?'

Mouse gave him her I-could-kill-you-right-now glare. 'He's an employee of my sister's. He was supposed to be taking William home from school.'

'Oh, I expect William dragged him in here to see Granddad!' She was smirking at the kid now, like Fee had done. Why did adults get in kids' faces like that? Walt remembered his Auntie May used to do that. Come to think of it, she looked like Auntie May, this manager, all tucked in about the middle, as if someone had once complimented her on a trim waist and she'd worn little belts and fitted skirts ever since. 'But I'm afraid we have security procedures, Mr . . . '

He didn't enlighten her and she went on, 'You never signed in and you appear to have been abusive to a member of my staff.'

'Abusive?' He stepped forward, stretching to his full height.

Mouse murmured his name like a warning. She was checking her father's wet shirt.

'You told her she wasn't doing her job properly.'

'You think that was abusive?' His face felt like stone. The sulky girl, Michaela, hurried between them with the mop. 'You should be fucking ashamed, leaving old folk to rot like this.' He swept an arm towards the residents. The old lady in the brown wig was laughing. Mouse's father was struggling to get out of his chair; she was rubbing his shoulder, trying to calm him.

'If Maura has a problem with her father's care that's up to . . .'

'Like Maura's going to complain. She has no choice but to leave him here, and you bloody well know it. What is it, a thousand quid a week to feed them out-of-date bread and then you can't even be arsed keeping 'em clean.' Rage was welling up inside him, filling the space behind his eyes, and this smug woman was still smirking at him.

'Robert!' Mouse grabbed his arm. 'Enough. Don't make it any worse. Go outside and I'll speak to you later.' Her jaw was so tight she could barely get the words out and her eyes were wet. He felt sorry then, and the fight went out of him. He shrugged off her hand and pushed his way out, knocking into the mop bucket so that dirty water slopped all over the linoleum.

26

They exited in silence, the door held open for them by Fee. She was a regular girl guide. She'd make a good psychologist, Walt thought. She already had the smile and the professional head tilt, the one that said, 'Don't worry, we can work on that next session.'

William began whining as soon as they hit the street. He was too hot, with the big parka. He was hungry, could they get chips? No one spoke. Walt risked a glance at Mouse's profile; she looked like she was walking on thorns. Cars streamed past and the pavement was crowded; office workers hurrying home and school kids loitering outside the supermarket. Walt led the way through a small gang of lads who were spraying Coke on squealing teenage girls.

'Can I go into the charity shop?' William said. He was peering in the smeared window of a bric-a-brac store. The mannequins were dressed in vintage leather and paisley scarves, and behind them, second-hand bookshelves displayed all the funny little things the kid liked: old tins, clunky watches, plastic animals. William pressed against the pane, making a triangle with his nose and palms, fogging up the glass in between them.

'No. We need to get home.'

When he didn't move, Mouse seized one skinny wrist, tugging his hand so he had to follow her. He walked slowly, eyes down, as if paddling in the sea. Walt lagged behind, watching the close-knit outline of the two of them. Mouse's hips swayed under the blue coat. He imagined her outrage if she figured out he was looking. He liked to see heels on a woman, but Mouse wore staid ankle boots, flat and a little scuffed. She didn't give a rat's ass about fashion, and he kind of liked that too. The on-going tension between them was pressing on his chest. He caught up with her. The lightest touch to her elbow and she turned to him, still walking.

'Maura, what I said back there – it needed saying.'

'You're always saying it, Mum,' William piped up from the other side. 'You're always saying they don't look after Granddad properly – his nails and stuff. And they make him wear other people's clothes.'

'I can fight my own battles, thank you. In a *tactful* way.'

'I don't do tact. I do justice.'

She stopped, right in the middle of the pavement. An old chap in a grey anorak swerved around her, tutting at her lack of direction. 'When I need your help, I'll ask for it.'

'Like today? No need to thank me for collecting your son from school.'

She shot him a venomous look. 'You messed that up too.' She turned, resumed walking, faster. William whined about his shoe and started hopping. She shook his arm. 'Stop that!'

'The kid wanted to see his granddad.'

'Oh, you think it's a good idea for him to see his granddad like that?'

'My shoes are too small. I need new shoes,' William said.

'That's life, isn't it? You can't protect him from everything.'

'I can try!'

'My toes are *really* sore.' William went even slower, until Mouse stopped again and looked down at the kid. Walt couldn't see her expression, but he was glad he wasn't the one on the receiving end.

'You are not getting new shoes, William. I know it's because you want the boxes.'

'I've got nine boxes.' His voice was low, sulky. 'I need ten.'

'You don't need ten.'

'I like ten. It's a good number.' He raised his voice, overtook his mother just a little so he could look across her disapproval at Walt. 'Walt, do you have any shoe boxes?'

'I don't buy shoes much.'

There was a brief silence.

'What about socks? Do you just buy one sock at a time?'

'William, that's rude!' his mother said.

'How is it?' Walt said. 'I've only one foot. The kid's being logical, and you're being overprotective again.'

'And you're being a pain in the arse!'

'Mum!' William dropped her hand. They'd reached the pedestrian crossing. They stood there uneasily, Mouse and William in front, Walt a step behind. He was flanked by a pensioner with a shopping trolley who smelled of mint and, on the other side, a mother with a little girl in a pink jacket and woolly hat. The child was standing next to William. They traded glances like two Jack Russells, and William's eyes dropped to her daisy-patterned wellingtons. Walt suppressed a smile; he could almost see the cogs turning. They must have come in a big box.

The green man flashed up and the crossing signal beeped. Everyone obediently stepped out onto the road. Walt waited until they'd reached the other side before speaking again.

'That fat lassie, she was away to give your dad a full cup of scalding tea. He'd have spilled it over himself.'

'So you managed to do that for him.'

'He knocked it out my hand. Where's the common sense? Expecting a frail old man to manage a full cup of tea.'

'He's not even that old!' That was wrung from deep down. Her tone softened. 'He's not even seventy. It's so unfair.'

A woman with a child in a pushchair navigated around them and they were forced to move closer together. Mouse smelled of fabric conditioner, not peachy perfume like her sister.

Tom's dad used to kid on that he grew peaches in his greenhouse, and they believed him. He gave away stacks of them in brown paper bags. It was years later that Walt discovered Tom's dad had a mate with a fruit stall in Jesmond. He and Tom and Steven would gorge themselves on peaches and make themselves sick. A little peach goes a long way.

'When was he diagnosed?'

'I'm not sure. I didn't have any contact with him for a while. I would meet Mum for a coffee now and again. She was desperate to see the baby, of course.'

Their pace had slowed, as if they were no longer in a hurry to get anywhere.

'Mum never let on there was anything wrong. She made herself ill trying to cope alone. Alys was down in London at that time, doing an internship in a gallery. Mum phoned me in the small hours one night. Dad had flushed his pyjama bottoms down the toilet and flooded the place and that was the final straw for her. She broke down on the phone and I had to get dressed and wake William up and get a taxi over to Fife. It was awful.' She glanced down at her son. 'I ended up staying with her, but Dad was a nightmare. He kept wandering. Twice we had to get the police. One time they found him at the station, waiting for the London train.'

A bouncer type in tracksuit bottoms muscled between them, so that Walt lost the thread of her voice. William was quiet, taking in this new drip-drip of information. 'His GP managed to get him into an assessment ward, but Mum had a heart attack three days later.'

He didn't need to ask whether it was fatal. Alys came back, she said, wanted everything tied up as quickly as possible. The castle was sold, and they moved their father into this home in Stockbridge. It was close to the Victorian townhouse Alys had set her sights on. Alys rarely visited him, though. She wasn't good around illness.

'So the money from the sale . . . ?'

'All Alys's. My father had cut me out of the will before his diagnosis.' Her chin jutted. Defiance, perhaps, or just the sort of pain that stiffens every part of you.

'You didn't contest it?'

'What's the point?' She sounded weary. 'Alys was happy for me to move in with her. It saves her having to do anything, make any decisions. She needs me, and she pays Dad's fees.'

He wasn't quite sure what to say.

'So if you've fallen out with your father, why visit him now?'

'You mean now he's unable to remember what we fell out about? Why do you think?'

He wanted to know what could be so bad that your own father would turn his back on you. Was it just that she had fallen pregnant? He thought of his own father, scurrying to his shed at the first hint of a raised voice. Like the time Walt had written off the family Toyota. Or the night he got pissed and punched a hole in the wall; then his Dad had gone to ground, emerging from his larchlap bunker only when the dust had settled. When Walt rowed with his mother there was a lot of fall-out – tight lips and long silences, the odd slammed door – but with his dad . . . There'd never been a cross word between them. They resolved things with a couple of cans in front of the telly and that was it.

'*He* fell out with *me*.' Mouse said, as if that explained it. 'By the time I made contact with him again, it was too late. He'd already been diagnosed.'

Guilt. He knew the symptoms, knew how she'd probe the feeling like a bad tooth until it hurt. She probably bought her father shirts he'd never wear, rich desserts from Marks & Spencer. There'd be lavender heat packs and wine gums, and when the old man swore at her and threw his juice across the room, she'd soak it up, like she somehow deserved it.

Walt knew about guilt. A young woman with a clipboard and serious spectacles had told him that he had survivor's guilt. *Recognising your good fortune doesn't diminish your sorrow and grief over the ones you have lost.*

After Tom, well-meaning people told him he'd been lucky. The 'lucky' word became a boulder, sitting in the pit of his belly.

He'd tried lots of things to dissolve it, like booze and weed. He'd driven fast cars late at night. Getting blown up, on that last tour, that had chipped a few lumps off the damn thing. Tom would have laughed at that.

But mostly, it was immovable. You just had to find a way to live with it. Or not.

He cleared his throat. 'Guilt is something you do to yourself,' he said gently.

She looked about to deny it; she would never sabotage herself in that way. 'I just do what I can,' she whispered eventually.

'These places, they know that. It's bollocks. That's how they make wads, out of guilt. Out of people like you, Maura, just trying to do what they can.'

It wasn't much of a thing to say, after she'd trusted him with all that family stuff, but it was how he felt. She gave him what his mother would have called an old-fashioned look.

'Why are you suddenly calling me Maura? You've done it three times now.' Her cheeks had gone pink, because he now knew she'd been counting. 'My family call me Mouse.'

'I'm not family. I'm just your sister's employee,' he reminded her. They'd reached Alys's front steps. William hopped up them, two at a time, pinched toes forgotten. They paused at the bottom of the steps, Mouse with her hand on the rail.

'I don't know what you are to me,' she said quietly. Something shimmered between them, a delicate filament of cobweb on the breeze. He thought he saw his own heartbeat in her eyes. And then she turned and went into the building.

27

'I don't know you any more!' Jo had shouted. They'd been having a row, a blazing, drunken row after a night clubbing in Newcastle; the sort of row where words are hurled as brazenly as missiles. 'I don't know who you are!'

He thought afterwards that it was a cruel thing to say to a guy who didn't know himself. He was not the same. He was an imposter with a boulder in his belly. That was another thing she'd said, that Tom was always between them, and he'd sniped back, 'Don't give me that "there are three people in my marriage" shite,' in his best Diana voice. Not that there was any hope of a marriage. She'd returned the engagement ring, later, by post.

They'd been downing shots in some bar near the station: bright blue ones, the colour of eyes. Tom's eyes. As the medic had worked on him, Walt had held his gaze gently in his, partly because he was scared to look at the place where Tom's legs had been. You'll be all right, bonny lad. We'll get you home. Trust me, I'll get you home, mate.

He swallowed blue shots until he couldn't remember the colour of his own eyes, and Jo had got that face on her, that scowl she saved just for him. Come on, she said, or we'll miss the last train back. He'd been living with her off and on in Morpeth at the time. She'd kicked off on the platform because he'd started up a bit of banter with some lasses on a hen night. It was the end of the night and their pink feathers were a bit bedraggled. Apparently he'd had more chat for the hens than he'd had for his fiancée all evening. He'd shaken off her hand, told her to fuck off in front of a platform of sniggering fellow drunks, and that's when she'd said she didn't know him any more.

The train had come in while they'd been arguing. The revellers had pressed towards it and Walt had stood there on the cold concrete, hunched into his thin jacket, rocking slightly on the balls of his feet. He might have left the best bits of himself in the desert. They might still be there, bloody fragments of compassion and decency stuck to the sand.

'Are you getting on?' she'd called, and he realised she was standing in the train carriage, looking out, doors wide open and the orange light behind her oddly welcoming. He couldn't move.

'Walt!' She hung on to the door, leaning out, and the guard came along and said, 'Step inside, love. Hands off the door.'

'But my boyfriend . . .'

'Are you getting on, sir?'

He couldn't move. The voices faded. He was aware of a shrill voice and the train doors closing and then the train pulled away in a cloud of fumes. He saw Jo's face, a white, angry blur pressed against the window.

'Are you okay? You don't look okay,' the guard had said.

He'd left the station, spent the night on a mate's sofa. An army mate, who understood.

28

Walt stood in the hall, level with the kitchen door. If he rocked forwards just a bit, making sure his shadow didn't betray him, he could see the two sisters. Alys was sitting at the table eating her breakfast, although it was after nine in the evening and William had already gone to bed. There was a family packet of cornflakes open beside her and she was ploughing through a heaped bowl of the stuff. Hot, milky tea steamed from her favourite mug, the one that said 'Taxidermists don't give a stuff'.

Mouse was scouring William's bright blue lunchbox in the sink. 'Dad was very upset today.'

'Yeah?'

'And then Walt turned up and things went from bad to worse.'

'Yeah.' Alys continued to chew, holding her spoon clumsily, the way a child would, at an unnatural angle. 'He does that. He upsets the balance.'

Mouse turned from the sink, wiping the plastic box with a tea towel. ' He's angry, I think. He always seems so angry.'

I'm not, I've never been angry, that's not me.

Walt slid back against the wall, trying not to meet Shackleton's accusing glare.

'He is cute, though, Walt.'

'Alys, don't say that.' There was a snapping noise. He could imagine Mouse folding her cloth in temper. 'That's not helpful. I don't know what to do about Dad.'

'We should get Weetabix. Will you get me some Weetabix, next time?'

Mouse sighed. 'Yes. Yes, I'll get some. Alys, I'm going out for my tea tomorrow. I'll defrost something for you.'

There was a silence: the kind that is way too silent.

'Where are you going?'

'Galen is taking me to that new bistro.'

'Galen?'

'Yes.'

'Galen? You shouldn't ever fuck your boss.'

'Don't be so crude. We're just going out for tea.'

'I don't want you to.' The sound of a petulant chair scraping back. 'You shouldn't get involved.'

'Alys . . .' A big gust of a sigh. 'It's just tea. Companionship.'

'That's not how he'll see it! Don't go. I don't want you to go.'

'Alys, I . . .'

There was a jarring crash, the sound of a cereal bowl being smashed to the floor. Walt slid down the wall, cradling his skull in his arms. The shattering radiated through his nervous system like red-hot needles. He could, vaguely, still make out Mouse's whispered promise: 'It's just a meal, Alys. I won't leave you.'

'Maybe we could swap mobile numbers,' Mouse said, the next day. 'Just for convenience.'

'It would be convenient . . . if I had one.'

'You don't have a mobile?' She looked at him in disbelief.

'No.' He thought of his nearly new iPhone. He'd left it on the table for his mother to find, and the act of setting it down, the finality of that dull metallic clunk, had remained with him like a taste in his mouth.

Her expression said 'that's odd', but she let it go. 'It doesn't matter. I'm just a bit paranoid, after my dad being upset like that. I don't know what triggered that.'

Coby. The word unpeeled in Walt's brain, but he came up with the thing you say in such circumstances. 'He's in the right place, you know.'

She did know. She said all the usual things people say in such circumstances: I couldn't look after him here; he needs proper nursing.

'He'll settle down,' Walt said. 'He'll be okay.' *Coby.* The word hovered between them, but, like the strange button, it was a thing best held back for now.

'Have you been in my room?' Walt fixed the kid with a hard stare.

'No.' Too quick, too sheepish.

'In my bag? Have you been in my bag?'

'No.' Even faster. William was studying the wall behind Walt. There was a downwards slant to his mouth and his eyes looked a bit shiny; Walt hoped he wouldn't cry. He hated weeping women and crying kids were worse.

'That's okay. I just thought . . . Ee, never mind.'

The kid ducked away.

Walt had been in his room earlier, folding up his clothes, putting his socks into a pile for washing. He had gone through his pack; it was a kind of ritual, a thing he did the way other people check for keys, change, their phone. This was all he had in the world now, this bag. Bergens had to be packed correctly, and always upright, so as not to disturb the layers. Heaviest items went at the bottom, jammed against the frame to protect your back: uniform trousers, or just jeans now, and then T-shirts. Socks and boxers went together at the top. The rope was old and had never lost its dampness. It was heavy, so it went at the very bottom. He checked it at least once a day, for security. When he'd checked that afternoon, the rope had shifted, as if someone had tugged at it. Walt had never moved it, or taken it out. It remained at the very bottom of the pack like a coiled snake, waiting. To check it was enough, for now.

29

The noose is tight around his neck, and the more his desperate fingers prise at the rope, the tighter it becomes, biting into his flesh. The weight of his body makes it worse. He is swinging from the tree, a dead weight. Breathing in short grunts, he jerks his legs, trying to break free. His skin is burning, caked in something black and treacly, clotting in lumps, and tough as concrete. Stuck to this are handfuls of feathers, soft, pretty, white ones. A single feather drifts weightlessly to the ground, curling like a new leaf. He tries to claw at the black, peeling it off in great strips that take his skin with it, until all that's left is his flayed body, still alive, bloody and jerking, hanging from the tree.

He came awake with a great gasp, like a man drowning, coming up for air. His heart was pounding. He was stuck to the sheets with dried blood. He wanted to scream but his tongue was paralysed, too big for his mouth. Slowly, slowly, he focused on the light creeping through the gap in the yellow curtains. White walls, white ceiling, cracks around the light fitting . . . And sweat, not blood, dampening the sheets.

He struggled to sit up and snap on the bedside light. Only those who have survived the dark know the comfort of a forty-watt bulb. *Christ.* He hid his face in his hands for a very long time, massaging the agitation from the tight lines around his eyes. A sigh shuddered through his whole body. Lowering his hands he reached over and tipped the alarm clock towards him. It was one of those old-fashioned travel ones, in a salmon-pink shell. Must have belonged to someone's granny. It was six in the evening.

It was the fucking birds that had done this.

He'd gone down to the basement looking for William. Mouse was making the tea and fretting. He shouldn't be down there, she'd said. What was he doing down there, when *Cash in the Attic* was on? Maybe he prefers watching *Death in the Basement*, Walt had joked, but she'd chosen to ignore that. He'd gone outside, made the familiar slog down the basement steps, through the silent, shivery shop. The animals, as always, watched his progress.

William was staring transfixed at something hanging from the beam.

It was a kebab of dead birds. They were strung up like onions in a gardener's shed, their plaintive beaks turned outwards, blue eyelids fine as tissue. A swarm of feathers; blue-black, charcoal, mud-brown. Walt spotted the orange-red bib of a young robin.

The stack of birds, the shape they made, and all those feathers . . . He'd served with an old-timer who'd been in Northern Ireland during the Troubles. The lad had seen a girl stripped once, in Belfast, for consorting with a British soldier. Her head had been shaved and she'd been covered in tar and feathers and tied to a tree. This anecdote had stayed with Walt for years, superseded by a more recent catalogue of horrors, but still there at the back of his subconscious. It was the feathers; how something so soft and pale and bonny could be used to crucify someone.

He'd told William to come on upstairs, his mam was looking for him. He wanted to push him towards the exit. William, soft and pale and bonny, should not be contaminated by Alys's world.

He hadn't felt like any tea, just went up to his room. 'It's shepherd's pie,' Mouse had called after him as he trudged up the stairs, not believing anyone could resist. He'd pulled over the curtain and lain down on his bed, enjoying the cool comfort of the quilt.

Until he'd fallen asleep.

30

He'd come down to the kitchen to raid the fridge and found William and his mother zipping themselves into their coats. There was a suppressed fizz of excitement about them that made him sad.

'You can come with us!' William bounced up to him. 'We're going to see the *Field of Light.*'

Walt risked a glance at Mouse. Her face was carefully neutral. 'What's the *Field of Light* when it's at home?'

The kid inhaled an important breath. 'It's in a square and it has nine thousand five hundred lightbulbs and you can walk through it!'

'It's an installation,' Mouse said. She was pulling on a knitted cap, self-consciously rearranging stray strands of fringe. She looked lovely, and he wanted to tell her that.

'Installation, my arse,' he said.

'Robert! Watch your language.'

William giggled. 'Please come with us. Can he come with us, Mum?'

'It doesn't sound like he wants to.' Mouse turned her back, gathering up her purse, her keys.

'I just don't get modern art. Look what it does to your sister.'

Mouse spun around and fixed him with a cold stare. 'Sometimes I think you think too much. Do you want to come with us or not?'

He nodded. She made a mocking after-you gesture towards the door.

They set off towards town, William moaning that it was too far to walk and couldn't they get a taxi?

'He's been in a taxi *twice*,' Mouse said, 'and now he thinks it's the only way to travel.'

'Walking takes too *long!*' William whined. They played a game of spotting green cars, and Walt won, although Mouse was called in to rule whether metallics could be taken into account, because some of the metallic greens were closer to turquoise.

'Do you even get turquoise cars?' said Walt.

'I think you do.' Mouse smiled to herself. 'I remember my dad had an old Rover – it was a pale turquoise, like the sea.'

'Now you're getting too poetic!' Walt grinned at her and she grinned back.

They crossed at the lights, turned onto George Street. It was dusk, and the place was illuminated by street lamps, mock Georgian lanterns in mock Georgian pubs, and cordons of fairy lights in beer gardens. Edinburgh was hopefully continental. Mouse pointed out the posh hotel where she'd had her twenty-first, and the pub where Galen had taken her for tea.

Walt raised an eyebrow and paused to look at the menu in the window. 'Pricey.'

'I'm worth it.' Mouse shot him a look beneath her lashes. His face slid into a smile. They walked on, William in the middle, humming to himself and hopping over the cracks in the pavement.

'Well, isn't this cosy!'

A small figure came up behind them. Mouse's pal Fee, in an oversized hat and scarlet lipstick. Mouse didn't say much; she looked like she was blushing. Did Fee think they were an item? He suddenly felt that tiny tweak of possibility you get on a first date.

Fee was meeting friends in the Café Royal. She was late, she said, and hurried away with the smug, knowing look of someone who doesn't know very much at all.

'Oh, great,' Mouse sighed, after she'd gone. 'Now it will be all round the shop. My secret date!'

Walt laughed at her expression. 'It'll ruin your chances with the old man!'

The *Field of Light* was set up in St Andrew's Square. They couldn't see anything at first, just the tall dark column in the centre of the garden. There were too many folk milling about – Japanese tourists with camera phones and suited youths wandering round with Starbucks – but then the path cleared and they found themselves surrounded by swathes of swaying, coloured spheres.

He remembered being ankle-deep in snowdrops. He was barefoot, at a time when he had two feet and could feel the soft tickle of petals between his toes. There was something about petals against your skin, and the fragrance of dark green, growing things, that made his head spin. He'd dropped to one knee and Jo had laughed and cried at the same time, tried to pull him up, but ended up pushing him down and they'd lain in a pool of damp whiteness and she'd said yes in a voice that he could still hear. The light had faded without them noticing. The trees sort of hung there, suspended between light and dark, and the snowdrops became luminous, like hundreds of eerie little nightlights.

The *Field of Light* made him think of those snowdrops.

'Wow!' Mouse was laughing as the colours rainbowed across her skin. The garden was blooming with alien seed pods, shifting like poppy heads in the breeze. William gripped the fence, suddenly silent. Walt rubbed his shoulder. 'You like?'

'It's awesome!' He turned around with a toothy smile, and then he was off, running through the crowded paths as if he could take in every sight and sound and colour in one go.

'William!' Mouse called after him.

'He's fine,' Walt said. 'He knows where we are.' His hand was on her back. It had been an unconscious gesture. Had she noticed? If he jerked it away, she would notice. He kept it there. They strolled along the path, slowly, gazing at the scintillating lights. Walt's hand grew warm. Mouse remained quiet. They came to a stop near the column.

'The artist was inspired by the heat and the light in the Red Desert, Australia,' she said.

'It looks like snowdrops to me. Lit from the inside.'

'Now who's a poet?' She turned to him, having to look up because he was so close and much taller. He could see the spheres like tiny diamonds reflected in her eyes. Reluctantly he let his hand drop from her back.

'Why snowdrops?'

'I proposed to my girlfriend in a snowdrop wood, at dusk.'

She looked shocked, almost; he wasn't who she thought he was. William came running back, counting out loud. She ignored him. 'What was her name?'

'Jo.'

'So you're married?'

He gave a sharp huff of a laugh. 'She broke it off. Wise girl.'

'Was that because of . . .' She glanced down, embarrassed.

'No. I still had two good legs then. It was just my mind that was fucked. Sorry.' He patted William's head.

The kid was still bouncing. 'I counted a hundred!'

'Well, keep going. Try the other side,' said Walt, deadpan.

The boy took off.

Mouse had turned back to the lights. Her hair was like fire in the strange glow. 'No one's ever asked me to marry them, and I've got a kid.'

He'd been looking over the fence, suddenly seeing not the ethereal buds of light, but the dark underbelly, the displaced earth, the tangle of wires. He felt the earth tilt a little, the familiar hot soak of fear. His belly clenched. *Don't let it destroy you. Don't.*

Stiffly he dropped to one knee, his good knee, with one hand on the fence, and when she looked around there was space where he should have been.

'Walt? Walt!' She grabbed his shoulders. A camera flashed nearby. 'Get up!'

'Maura, will you do me the honour of . . .'

'Walt!'

A knot of people had gathered. There was a cry of 'go on yersel', big man!' Three excited Japanese schoolgirls brandished their smartphones.

'. . . of becoming my . . .'

William had returned and stood rooted to the spot, saucer-eyed. Mouse was laughing, pulling at Walt's jacket. 'Get up, you moron!'

'. . . wife! Will you marry me, Maura?' The crowd cheered. 'Jesus, me knee! Help me up.'

She grabbed his arm and hauled, and the two of them half collapsed together, giggling.

Walt ruffled her fiery hair. 'I'm sorry. Couldn't resist it.' He placed a soft kiss on her cheek. 'That's what happens when you don't think too much.'

31

It's one of life's little jokes that men wake up every morning with an erection and an urgent need to pee. For Walt, there was a third phenomenon: an irrational fear that bloomed in his belly every night. Sometimes his bad dreams were shot to hell on waking, reduced to blurred frames he'd learned not to splice together. But the residue remained. The answer was to get out of bed, to get moving, shift the fear still fluttering inside like a trapped moth.

That Sunday morning, the fear had a warm fuzzy edge. He noticed it because it was so unexpected. Lying in bed he ran over the events of the previous evening like a drunk hunting for flashbacks, but he could find no cringe-worthy moments, no skeletons. It had been good.

They'd left the square and ended up in a fast-food place, eating ketchupy burgers under cheap fluorescent lights. Walt had apologised. It wasn't up to Galen's standard, and Mouse was surely a soft-music-and-candlelight sort of girl. She'd chuckled and scored him five out of ten. William had given him an eight, on account of the free gift that came with the meal. The lad had constructed a bright yellow plastic car as they chatted away like normal people. Walt had spoken about Jo, and his parents, and Mouse had told him more about the castle and her father's illness. Not earth-shattering revelations, just the humdrum yellow plastic parts that make up your life. It felt good.

'Is Galen taking you out again?' Walt had wanted to know, and Mouse had shrugged, as if she didn't much care. It was probably a mistake, she'd said, to get involved, especially when she had zero feelings for the guy. William had left them briefly at that point to go to the toilet, trundling the little car along with him. Walt had looked at her across the table and said, 'There needs to be a bit of chemistry. Find someone who sets your heart racing.'

And she'd opened her mouth to speak, and closed it again, as if there wasn't any point in saying what she was about to say. She'd looked down at her hands, and he'd looked at them too, at the smooth skin and the blunt, no-nonsense nails, and he'd fought the urge to take hold of them. Suddenly William was back, leaning against the Formica table, his expression filled with urchin-like pathos, a Victorian painting of a lost boy.

'Walt,' he'd said quietly. 'The bogs in here are just fucking shite.'

Walt grinned, remembering. The warm fuzziness settled over him like a net. He was getting too close to Mouse. Couldn't stop thinking about her, the thought of her igniting a weird mix in the pit of his stomach, a fierce cramp of joy and longing. Homesickness with the possibility of home.

He talked himself out of it, of course. He was just passing through. Mouse was a bitch, a shrew, saddled with a bairn and that sister . . . There wasn't any possibility that he'd want to get involved. She would be needy too. Maybe just wanting a father for the kid or someone to cut the grass. Nah, there was no way he'd want to get involved – and yet. And yet . . .

He loved the soft sweep of her cheek, the way her eyes went all misty when he made her laugh. He wanted to take hold of her square, capable hand, feel the texture of her hair. The coyness of his thoughts made him cringe. What the fuck was wrong with him? Back in the day any woman he met was fair game. If he thought about them at all, it was on a porn loop in the sleazy private recesses of his brain; but something stopped him thinking like that about Mouse, about *Maura*. Oh, he could imagine it, being in bed with her, naked. Could anticipate how her skin would feel, about how they would move together, fit together, the soft sounds she might whisper . . .

Shit. He checked the clock. It was nine thirty and he thought he could smell coffee and toast, but that might have been wishful thinking. He wanted to imagine Mouse waiting for him downstairs, a smile in place. In his imagination it was just the two of them, a normal warm fuzzy Sunday.

But this was Alys's house.

Cursing, he rolled to the edge of the bed, leaned over and grabbed his prosthesis. In the bathroom, he shuffled uncomfortably; it was always freezing in there. He ran water into the sink but it was slow to come hot. Alys had a thing about conserving energy, turning down every appliance in the house. He drenched his face with icy water, coming up slowly, glistening, to peer at himself in the mirror. When he first came out of hospital, he'd done a lot of peering into mirrors. He'd never been one for all that metrosexual stuff: the hair gel and the moisturiser and so on. The most he'd ever admired his reflection was when he was all kitted out in his dress uniform, before a regimental dinner or something. He'd looked at himself with pride, for the man he was, his integrity, his resourcefulness. It had never been about appearance. When he'd come home though, without his foot, he'd had to steel himself to look. But actually, the foot was just surface. He'd taken to searching his face in the mirror for the evidence of how he felt inside.

Melissa, the art therapist, had once shown him some photographs of frontline troops: 'before and after' shots. He'd looked at them for a long time, staring into eyes that had seen too much. He wondered if his eyes looked like that to other people. Did Mouse see blue irises and black lashes? Or did she see the bruising shadows underneath that never went away? His 'after' face was leaner, anything soft and fleshy stripped away along with his peace of mind.

What was going on inside didn't have a reflection.

When he came down the stairs, Alys was sitting on the bottom step in the shadow of the great polar bear. Shackleton made her look tiny, like something out of Narnia. He paused on the half landing where the stair turned, his gut was already clenching. What did this mean? Only her back was visible to him, the long sweep of her spine, a twist of hair, unwashed. Her backside looked childishly narrow perched on the stairs. She was wearing mismatched pyjamas: the top a washed-out pink, the bottoms stamped with purple butterflies. He thought of the butterflies pinned to the beams in her studio. She didn't look back when he resumed walking, just tilted her head, as if she was listening. She spent far too much time with birds.

'If this is a *joke*,' she said, 'it isn't funny.'

Mouse's laptop was open on the kitchen table. William was hunched over it, his face washed-out and baggy in the blue light from the screen. His mother was standing behind his chair, arms folded, leaning in. She was biting her lip. They both looked up when Walt came in.

'What's wrong with her?' He jerked his head back towards the hallway.

'Oh, this is just great,' Mouse said, flinging up her hands. 'Just great.'

William said, uncertainly, 'Mum has been tagged in a post, Walt.' Walt crossed the space between them, heart hammering. 'What post? What do you mean?' They stood in silence, staring at the screen. Walt didn't know what he was supposed to be looking at. His eyes scanned over a jumble of meaningless photos until Mouse's name jumped out at him. There was a line of writing, just one sentence bookended with smiley faces and champagne glasses: 'Maura, you kept this quiet!'

Next to it was a little image of Fee, pouting in her trendy specs. There was a fuzzy picture below, with a 'play' button in the centre.

'You're all over Facebook, Walt,' the kid said solemnly, as he clicked on the button.

Suddenly, horribly, that stupid, impetuous marriage proposal burst into life. There was Walt in St Andrew's Square, down on one knee, the *Field of Light* swaying gently behind him, and Mouse giggling. You could hear her saying, 'Walt! Get up, you moron!' Behind them, the Japanese girls were clicking away on their phones. Fee must have seen it too, and decided to film the whole thing, sharing the happy moment with the whole fucking Facebook universe.

'Shit!' Walt scraped back his hair with both hands, holding onto his scalp. 'Who can see that? Can anyone see it? Delete it. Just delete it.'

'I'm not sure how.' William shrugged.

'Then find out!'

'Don't shout!' Mouse squared up to him. He hadn't realised he'd been shouting. He turned away, crossing his arms over his chest. He felt sick. He'd been so careful. He'd left his phone at his mother's, paid for things in cash so there'd be no electronic trail. And now here he was on Facebook, proposing in an Edinburgh square. What if it went viral? Steven was on Facebook.

'Alys saw it,' Mouse was saying. 'She was horrified. She seems to think you two are an item. I tried to explain it was a joke but . . .' She pressed a hand across her lower face. Her eyes seemed huge, fixed on the screen 'I tried to tell her it was a joke.'

'She doesn't do jokes.' Walt was pacing. He had to go, get out of here.

'She's very literal.'

'So are most people.' He came back to the table. 'We need to get that off there. Fast.'

Mouse reared back to look at him, and he moved away from her questioning eyes, started to fill the kettle, playing for time. He wanted to bang his head against the cupboard door.

'I've already made tea,' she said. Her voice was clipped. 'There's a full pot of it on the table.'

'Oh, because tea will fix everything.' He slammed off the switch and turned to face her again.

William, oblivious, was trawling for videos of cats and dogs.

'Don't take it out on me! You were the one acting the idiot!' They stood glaring at each other over the kid's head. Alys wandered back in, all little girl lost in her mismatched pyjamas. She paused for effect at the other side of the table. Walt could not escape her gaze. It peeled away his veneer, exposed the bits he wasn't proud of.

'I thought you liked me,' she whispered. 'I thought we were getting close.'

He opened his mouth to deny it, but Mouse said, 'I told you not to mess with her, didn't I? I told you to keep your distance.'

'And now you want to marry my sister!'

'No, I don't! I don't want to be close to anybody! I should never have come here.' This burst from him, surprised him. 'You know what? I quit – the job, the house, this whole fucking family.'

William was staring at him, but he knew better than to catch his eye.

Mouse made a little, satisfied noise in her throat: *hmm*. I knew this would happen, that's what she was thinking. The room was suddenly too small. He felt like thumping someone, was dizzy with the redness.

'When did you decide to marry?' Alys said, as if he hadn't spoken. She stepped forward, picked up the teapot and began to pour a thin trickle into her red mug. It had never been a good pourer, that teapot. And it was heavy. He could see the sinews in her wrist popping with the strain. Her pulse fluttered among the blue veins like a bird's heart. No one answered her.

Then William piped up: 'Look, Auntie Alys. There are loads of jokes on here, like puppies falling asleep in their food bowls. And cats. Lots of cats.' His voice was soft and wheedling, the sort of voice he might have used to call a truce in the playground. 'Pax', that's what they said in Walt's day. Shout 'pax' and everything stops, all the pushing and shoving and hostage-taking. Everyone is disarmed, for just that millisecond of peace.

Pax.

Walt tried to slow his breathing. Alys was still holding the teapot. She looked at him again, skinned him. He felt the chill on his innards. Her face was calm, a mask. And then she let go of the teapot.

Thank God you were there, said Mouse afterwards. Thank God.

It was nothing, he'd said. I've got quick reactions.

She hadn't dropped the teapot, Alys. Hadn't thrown it. She'd just abandoned it. As it fell, Walt reacted. *Hypervigilance*. He'd grabbed William, hoisted him off the chair. The pot crashed onto the table and split apart, a tide of scalding tea seeping around the laptop and soaking the seat where William had been sitting.

Alys had left the room without looking back.

Mouse had taken up William and hugged him until Walt thought they might both fracture, like the teapot. He watched from the sidelines.

'I'd worry about Alys,' he said eventually, 'if I were you.'

32

That night, he kept waking up with the past in his head; not the nightmarish parts, just the what-ifs that littered his path like cigarette butts. He kept thinking of Jo. Perhaps he was just horny. He switched on the lamp beside his bed and lay staring at the cracks in the ceiling.

Jo was with someone else now, according to Steven. In the hospital she'd visited him once, but they'd already broken up by then, so it was more of a courtesy call. She'd had a lucky escape from all the rehab and the medics and the rebuilding. She'd brought him grapes (original) and a bottle of elderflower cordial. 'I love the taste, it reminds me of spring,' she'd said, as she poured him a glass.

It had been spring when he'd proposed to her. She'd picked a clutch of snowdrops and carried them back to their hotel room like a bride in training, and somehow left them lying on the bed. When Walt had seized her and kissed her and urged her down onto the fresh sheets, the crushed white scent of snowdrops had clung to their bare skin for hours. They'd lain together like two saplings, legs spiralled, talking about the future on the same pillow. They shared the same looks, Jo and himself: both tall and straight, the same unruly dark hair, although his had been cut short back then. Nose to nose, it was like looking into a mirror, breath misting dark blue eyes. He chose to inhabit a little bubble, not looking forward, trying not to look back. They carried that small patch of woodland around with them for months, intoxicated.

On his next tour, the imaginary wood was his happy place. It was untouchable, a sanctuary, and when he fucked Jo in his memory, that glorious moment of entering her smelled always of fresh spring green.

And then Tom got blown up, and the wood became a wasteland overnight.

Somewhere in the small hours, he must have fallen into a deep sleep, because he was jolted out of it by the sound of his door clicking open. He lay rigid, waiting for his body's manic downloading of data to subside. The light was still on. There was no one there. Cursing, he heaved himself from the bed on his one leg, leaning on the bedside cabinet for support. He hefted the door shut, displacing a puff of chilly air, which smelled faintly of onions. He got back into bed. There's no one there, he kept repeating to himself. No one there. It's the faulty catch on the door. He kept meaning to wedge the damn thing shut. This was about the third time it had sprung open of its own accord, leaving him in a state of panic.

He dozed for another hour, before finally giving up and swinging his legs out of bed. He reached for his prosthesis, went through the motions of securing it. First the liner, the all-important second skin, which protected his residual limb, then the moulded resin socket. It was a snazzy blue – matched his eyes, the physio had joked. The foot was carbon: a flexible, all-terrain jeep of a foot. A go-anywhere foot. It was funny how quickly it had become a part of him. He'd assimilated it. His mind, on the other hand, was a thing apart: floundering, ungainly and damaged.

Finally, he stood up tall, worked the kinks from his back, and strode over to the window. The curtains were stained yellow by the streetlights. Drawing aside one half, gently, like a bride's veil, he gazed down onto the dark street. He could get dressed, take up his pack and simply walk out. It was easy done. Sighing, he rested his brow against the cold glass. He'd tried so hard to make a clean break. They would never have traced him. He could have remained here, concealed, for ages, or travelled north, inflicted himself on some other unsuspecting family. But now it was all fucked up. He'd gone viral. How long before one of Steven's sprogs, swiping through his iPad, came across Uncle Robert on Facebook? How fucking long?

He walked over to his pack and began to check it. Light things at the top: boxers, T-shirts. Heavier things at the bottom: jeans. Rope.

33

Should he leave a note?

They always did, in films. It would be better than a half-empty Scotch bottle. More dignified. He had a note already, didn't he? The death letter, the one they make you write, saying goodbye to your nearest and dearest. He hadn't needed to use it before. Maybe it would find its purpose now. He'd find a place for it, propped up against the sugar bowl.

It hadn't travelled well: there was a coffee ring across the corner, which seemed a bit cavalier. If your mother was to receive a goodbye note, it should be pristine, like a well-starched handkerchief.

Walt takes a last swig of whisky; places the tumbler beside the bottle. Next to that he leaves his keys and his mobile phone, arranging them carefully for no obvious reason, trying not to imagine his mother picking them up, turning on the phone to ring him in that muddled way she acts around technology.

He takes a last, long look around the kitchen: at those awful curtains with the big sunflowers, as familiar as his own clothes; the drawer with the missing handle that Dad has never fixed; the spice jars lined up in a special pine rack, even though Mam only ever uses salt and pepper and maybe the odd bay leaf. Realisation seeps through his fuddled brain. This is the end of the road, my friend. The End.

He's always liked the garden in the half dark. He likes the sounds and the tired smells: damp flowers, woodsmoke, a soupçon of fried onions left over from teatime. He remembers the boy hiding in the apple tree, and as he climbs the drainpipe it's as if the boy is watching him, hiding in the foliage of the past. Walt has lost sight of himself now, but the boy can see him. The boy watches him unbind the washing line from the gutter, working it between his fingers until the hemp strafes his cold cuticles; but on he labours, as if there's a lot riding on the untying of the rope. He can almost hear gunfire. The cowboys are lynching their man and the boy is whispering in his ear, 'They pee themselves when they're hanged.' At last the rope is free and coiled round his elbow like a skein of wool as he strides towards the tree. The ancient knot is knitted into the bark and the tree still seeps around the wound. Walt tugs the rope, testing the tension, and the boy repeats, 'They pee themselves, you know.' That is the only thing he is afraid of.

34

As Walt crept from the bedroom, he sensed he wasn't the only one up.

William was sitting on the bottom step of the attic stair, shoe-boxes fanned out across the landing carpet like tarot cards, lids carefully tucked beneath them. He was hunched over, his face furrowed with the effort of thinking. His eyes looked pouchy, the soft skin underneath stained violet. He jumped when Walt spoke.

'What you doing, son? It's not even light outside.'

'Something woke me up.'

'What?'

'I thought . . . dunno.'

'Did you open my door a while back?'

The kid's head shot up. 'No. Why?'

'Nothing. Just a faulty catch. What are you doing now?'

'I'm sorting my boxes into colours. Look.'

William beckoned him over. The first box on the left contained all things yellow and orange. He had peach raffle tickets in there, a pencil stub, yellow plastic sunglasses and a carton of sandalwood joss sticks he'd pinched from his auntie. He poked through the second box, obviously blue; there were his mother's turquoise beads, a postcard from the Med, a small blue ceramic starfish. Walt's gaze roamed over the boxes: red, green, grey and so on. It was all a bit obsessive.

Walt wondered what Mouse made of it all, and experienced a dart of something fearful. He opened the red box: an old lipstick, a marker, a diary with a wine leather cover. And underneath . . . He grabbed the stiff peak of a cap and pulled it out; items rolled to the floor and William squeaked in protest. He examined the cap, held it under his nose. It smelled faintly of the basement and the odour made his stomach crawl.

'Where'd you get that?'

'It was just lying around.' William shrugged, defensive.

'It was lying around in the basement. Your mother said we should throw it out.' Walt held his gaze for a moment, but the kid was sharp, and quickly changed the subject.

'I have a black box,' he said. 'Do you want to see in the black box?'

Walt sighed. A black box. You just knew there had to be a black box. Carefully Walt lowered himself to the floor.

'Right, talk me through this one.'

As dawn streaked the sky behind the tenements across the street, Walt found himself sitting on the outside step. He'd lit a last fag, zipped up his too-thin jacket. The daylight settled in around him, moist with unshed rain. He would get a train, go north. He glanced at his pack, slumped against the railings. He had all he needed.

Or he could just walk to the park. One last time.

His thoughts jerked back to William and his magpie collection.

William had been keen to show off his treasures: an unwrapped, furry stick of liquorice toffee, a piece of sea-coal from Cramond beach, a ring with an onyx stone. *Does your mother know you've taken that?* A black plastic comb. A leather wallet and, deep inside it, a pile of monochrome snaps. Walt had taken them out and held them up in the lamplight. He recognised the backdrop – castle walls and stunted trees – from Mouse's descriptions of her childhood. There was even a tumbledown structure that may have been the cowshed-turned-garage. In one of the shots, two men, both in work gear, posed beside an old Ferguson tractor. Walt had traced a finger over the grainy image.

'Who's that?'

'My granddad,' William had said, pointing to the man on the left. He was stocky, with a dark moustache and a bold stare. Walt saw a faint shadow of the man in the care home; the strong bone structure, the large outdoor hands. The second man was shorter, slighter, with a prim smile. His nose and his lips gleamed with dots of light.

'And him?'

'That's Uncle Coby,' William whispered. 'But we don't talk about him.'

The front door banged, jolting Walt back to the present, to the cold stone beneath his backside. He fought the urge to hit the deck. *Hypervigilance.* Just go with it, the psychologist had advised. He'd talked about grounding techniques. *Hold on to something concrete. Rationalise your surroundings.* Stating the obvious was supposed to be some kind of a mantra to ward off flashbacks. When the past reached out to get you, just remind yourself, *this is Monday. I am sitting on the step. That's just the door banging, not a bomb.* He'd had a big problem with clapping in the early days. He'd been at one of the kids' birthday parties, and the applause that greeted the birthday cake had sent him ducking under the table. He was instantly in a ditch in Helmand, bullets cracking past his head. That was one way to spoil a party.

'Jesus! What are you doing out here?' Mouse was all belted up in the blue coat. He struggled to his feet.

'What are *you* doing out here?' he countered. 'Bit early for work, isn't it?'

'I just got a call from my father's care home. He's gone missing. Just walked out, sometime in the night.' Her voice was shaky.

'Shit.' He went to reach out a hand to touch her hunched shoulders, then thought better of it.

'Could you stay with William? He's playing in his room.' She looked guilty. 'I just have to go down and see what's going on. I left a note to say . . . I thought you were still in bed.'

Walt felt his throat tighten. 'Don't do this to me. I'm not a fucking babysitter. I won't always be here.'

'I know! I'm sorry. But it's too early to call Mrs Petrauska.'

'Don't ask me.' He grabbed his pack and headed down the steps.

'Don't do this to *me!*' Her anguish flowed after him. He paused, looked up. She was crying; standing at the top of the steps, tears running down her face. He sighed and turned back.

'Go on. Go on. Do what you have to do. I'll look after him.' He trudged back up the steps as she ran down. She grasped his arm briefly as she passed. He rested his brow once against the clammy door before letting himself back in. When he looked back, she was running down the street.

'Your father's gone missing from the care home.'

Walt thought he'd better say something. Mouse's note still sat on the table, but he doubted if Alys had read it. She was still in her pyjamas, staring into one of the freezer drawers as if she couldn't quite remember why she was there. She looked up at him, frowning.

'Really?'

'I said I'd stay with William.'

'Cool.' She turned back to the freezer.

He pulled a chair from under the table and sat down. No one had the right to be that neutral. He wanted to provoke a reaction, prod her with an imaginary stick until her scorpion tail revealed itself.

He had sat down at her place setting. He hadn't intended to, but there was a perverse enjoyment in it. He ran a finger round the rim of her red mug. 'Want a coffee?' he asked.

'Ugh. Can't stand coffee. Never drink it.'

Walt thought of the unexplained coffee he'd found before, but now wasn't the time to try and get answers from her.

'I expect he's wandering around in his pyjamas right now,

your dad,' he said. 'He'll be confused, in shock. Lost. And I think it's going to rain.'

Alys got up, balancing two wrapped packages in the crook of her wrist as she slammed the freezer door shut.

'I thought I had a waxwing,' she said, 'but I wasn't sure. They're quite hard to get, because they only winter here, on the east coast. I'm going to dress it as a highwayman. They have this black mask around their eyes.'

'Did you hear what I said, Alys? Your *father* is missing.'

'I heard you.' She approached the table. Her mouth had gone sullen, all tucked in, the bottom lip pouting. 'You're sitting in my seat. That's my mat and my mug.'

'For Christ's sake!' He scraped the chair back and got up. They were very close. He loomed over her, and it frightened him a bit, because he could feel his temper flaring. He gripped the edge of the table. *She's damaged, she's ill*, he kept repeating to himself. But she didn't *look* ill. He wanted to shake her like a cereal box until her flaws fell out, and then he might understand her better. She was looking up at him, and her eyes were cold.

'You don't know,' she said. 'You don't know what I've been through. My father was never there for me.'

And then she turned away. He grabbed her elbow, and one of the packages fell to the floor and burst open. A brittle, broken wing fanned out across the tiles. He stooped to pick it up, gently folding away the needle-like bones, the frozen feathers. When he straightened up, she was right there, in his face. He could smell peaches. She tucked a strand of hair behind one ear, licked her lips.

'No,' he said. 'No. It's not that I don't find you attractive but . . .'

Did he find her attractive? She scared him. Maybe the thrill was no more than that.

She didn't say anything. Her lip curled. She snatched the parcel and stalked off.

Walt upended the cereal box, shaking a generous portion of cornflakes into William's bowl. Had they always been bright yellow like that? No wonder kids were hyper these days.

'When I was a kid we got free toys in our cornflakes,' he said. God, he sounded like his dad. William was watching him intently, kneeling on the chair in his dressing gown, chin in his hands.

'Didn't you choke on them?'

'Nah, we didn't choke on anything in those days – it was before Health and Safety.' He plonked the bowl in front of the kid, steered the milk carton towards him.

'So don't I have to go to school today then?' William reached for his spoon.

Walt shrugged. 'Nothing was said. I'd wing it. Tell them there was a family emergency.'

'Well, it is an emergency, isn't it?' William chewed his lip.

'It's only an emergency if he's not found.' Walt wiped around the sink. 'He's probably sitting in the park.'

'It's raining.'

'So he'll get wet. He'll be fine, kid. Eat your flakes.'

'I can't.' William pushed away the bowl. 'I think we should go out and look for him.'

'That's not part of my remit.'

'I don't know what that means. I just want to go and look for my granddad. He'll be scared.'

Walt threw down the cloth. Jesus, this was exhausting. The phone rang and he picked up on the third ring. It was Mouse.

'They've called the police now. I insisted they call the police,' she said. 'You know, he's been missing since the middle of the night.'

'The police are involved?'

'Yeah, they came and asked loads of questions. I said he's a lost man in pyjamas, what else do you need to know?'

'What sort of questions?'

'Just about . . . What does it matter? What's wrong with you? Is William okay?'

'What do you mean what's wrong with me?'

'You sound weird.'

'You sound angry.'

'I am angry!' Her sigh gusted over the static. 'I knew this would happen. He's been agitated for days and the staff just don't take it seriously. Anyway, I've got to go. Is William okay? And where's Alys?'

'He's fine. Just having his breakfast, and Alys is away with the birds down in the basement. Maura, everything's fine. I'll ask Mrs Petrauska to stay with William.'

'That would be great.' Her voice softened.

He hated this. She wasn't really hearing him. She hadn't even clocked his rucksack leaning against the railings, that morning.

'Why don't you come here, to the home?' she said. 'They've left a policewoman here – she's coordinating the search.'

He didn't reply, just signed off with a mumbled goodbye and replaced the receiver.

'Right, kid. I'm going to ring Mrs P and then I'm going to . . . go.'

William's face crumpled. 'I want to go too. I hate being a kid.'

'Yeah, it sucks, but it won't last long.' He was already dialling Mrs Petrauska's number.

35

Mrs Petrauska arrived with a Tupperware box of vanilla pastries, as if she'd been sitting waiting for the call for hours. She was the sort of person who loved a good emergency.

'I told her zis would happen.' She touched her smooth brow with the back of her hand. 'A tragedy.'

'Not yet.' Walt waved her into a chair. 'Help yourself to tea or whatever. I'm going.'

'I have my own chamomile.' She patted her coat pocket. 'You go to search? They are lucky to have you, a soldier. So lucky!'

He swerved away from her smile. He met William's eyes as he took a last look around the kitchen. 'Be good, kid.'

He'd dumped the Bergen beside Shackleton, out in the hall. He grabbed it on the way past and let himself out silently into the daylight. The breeze was cool on his heated face. The rain had paused, but he could still smell it in the air, that taste of oppression. He hated thunder. It was worse than clapping.

He shouldered the pack, paused to light a fag, shielding the flame of his lighter from a sudden nip of cold air, eyes narrowing as the breeze whipped his own smoke back at him. He wondered where the police would search first. Probably the park, the banks of the river; all the places that would be most dangerous for an old guy in a state of confusion. He breathed out a ragged plume of smoke, slanting his face to the sky, and set off in the opposite direction.

As he walked, his thoughts turned to William's collection, to the black box. *Not your business now. Let it go.*

He thought about the strange collection of photographs. *We don't talk about Uncle Coby*.

Only someone was still talking about Uncle Coby. An old man, wandering lost and alone in the big city. Was he still calling?

He arrived at Waverley as the first peal of thunder rumbled in the distance. Was there safety in numbers? He joined the mêlée, and the thunder became lost in the underground rumbling of trains. He blended in, one of many guys in faded denim with rucksacks and grim expressions. Like them, he stared at the departure screens and prayed for a sense of direction. A pigeon fluttered down and landed beside his foot. Somewhere near the rafters, a precise, nasal female voice announced the train departures: 'The next train to depart platform nineteen is the eleven twenty-four to Dundee, stopping at Haymarket, Cupar and Leuchars.'

Dundee would do.

He automatically checked his left sock. The two twenties Alys had given him a few days earlier were still there, tucked in for safekeeping. Any wages had been erratic, but welcome. He had a stash of notes folded inside his boxers at the bottom of the pack, but he had no idea how long he needed that to last. Finding a job and a room in Edinburgh had been pure luck, and he doubted that luck would hold out. But there were hills above Dundee; if necessary he would buy a tent and hole up. He couldn't look beyond that.

A woman dragging a tiny suitcase on wheels banged into him, and he did that thing of apologising, even though he was the stationary one. He stepped back, realising he'd been staring at the departure screen for an unnaturally long time. His rucksack snagged on something. He apologised again, turned, and there was Galen. They both made surprised noises, and the pharmacist cleared his throat.

'Oh. Are you looking for Maura's father?'

'Are you?'

'Um, well, she phoned me about it, of course, but I'm afraid I'm off to a conference today. In York.'

Walt nodded, waiting for him to notice the rucksack. The guy was wearing the same sludge-coloured suit, with a slight flare to the trouser leg. His beard looked freshly cropped, and he was wearing rimless spectacles. Mouse had told him a funny thing about the glasses: they had a language all of their own. Perched on the end of his nose, he was waspish; on top of his head, distracted. If he took them off and chewed the leg, he was leading up to something.

Galen took off his glasses and peered at Walt with eyes that matched his general sludge-coloured appearance. Even his greying hair and beard carried a faint sandy hue.

'Are you going somewhere? Leaving in a hurry?'

The rucksack had been spotted. No hiding from Galen. Walt grunted something, and the guy tapped his front teeth with the tip of one spectacle leg. What the hell did that mean?

'It's a strange time to take off, isn't it?' he persisted.

'I'm going to visit a friend. In . . . the north.'

'Must be important, with Maura in the fix she's in.'

'Must be an important conference.'

'It is.' He bit down on the hard plastic. 'Look, it's none of my business, um, Walter, but I wouldn't like to see Maura . . . taken advantage of.'

'Me neither.' Walt looked him squarely in the eye.

The tannoy clicked and whined: 'The next train to arrive at platform ten is the eleven-fifteen to York.'

'Ah, that's me.' Galen hesitated, replacing his spectacles and checking for his ticket in the breast pocket of his jacket. 'So where are you going, in the north?'

Walt glanced up at the board above the platform barriers. 'Helensburgh.'

'That's west.'

'North-west.'

Galen tipped his glasses to the end of his nose. 'Well, you'd better go. That's your train, about to depart.'

'Plenty time. You'd better hurry though. Isn't platform ten across the other side?'

'Is it?'

'Yeah, you don't want to be late for your conference.'

'The train now arriving at platform ten is . . .'

'Oh, gosh.' Galen hitched up his briefcase and straightened his tie. He looked about to say something else, but instead hurried off with a mumbled goodbye. He was a man struggling with Something That Doesn't Add Up. Walt gave a grim smile. Fifteen minutes until the Dundee train. He wandered over to a kiosk selling coffee and bagels. The smell made his mouth water. There were two women in front of him, mother and daughter perhaps. The mother was jingling loose change in her hand. She was one of those tall, elegant types who look wealthy without trying: well-pressed slacks, lots of gold jewellery and a statement scarf. His mother hated scarves. She could never tie them properly, she said. They ended up knotted tight around her throat like a noose. He shivered.

'I think we should go back. Call someone,' the woman was saying.

The girl shrugged. She was young, heavily made up. 'He was a homeless.'

'*A* homeless? What kind of language is that?' Definitely her mother.

The girl lifted two cardboard cups from the counter and the mother paid. 'I'm just saying. You see them all over. He was probably just getting a heat.'

'I'm not surprised. He was in his pyjamas!'

They passed Walt in a drift of perfume.

'Yes, sir?' The barista looked at him hopefully.

'Um . . . I'll have . . . No, it's okay.' He turned and walked after the two women. 'Excuse me – the man in the pyjamas?'

They both stopped and looked at him as if he was barking, as if they'd never even mentioned pyjamas.

'I'm looking for someone. He's missing from a care home.'

'Oh dear.' The elegant woman put a hand to her neatly knotted scarf. 'Well, we saw a man in there.' She pointed to the central waiting room.

The girl nodded. 'He had an overcoat on, over his pyjama bottoms. And slippers, those leather ones. I thought they were shoes at first. We thought he was a homeless man.'

'*You* thought. *I* said we should call someone. Look, there's a policeman.'

Walt thanked them and ducked away.

The waiting room was crowded with tourists, all the benches taken. And then he spotted him, over to the side, next to a rubbish bin. He approached cautiously, as if the old boy might suddenly bolt.

'Hey, it's me . . .' He realised he didn't even know the guy's first name. Had anyone ever mentioned it? He'd become 'Mouse's dad' or 'William's granddad'. He groped around for a suitable form of address. 'Mr Morrison, it's me, Walt.'

The man looked up. His eyes were bright, but fearful. At some point in the night, he'd had the presence of mind to don an old mackintosh. It wasn't his; that much was obvious. It engulfed him, sagging from his shoulders and all but concealing his paisley-patterned pyjamas. This was probably why he'd gone undetected for so long. He looked shabby, out of it, a vagrant; the type of person no one wants to look at.

It was amazing that he'd managed to get this far. A place of movement and travel, of people going places. Had he made some kind of connection in his head? Walt imagined what it would be like to wash up here, amid the din, the chaos, the sheer press of humanity, and feel yourself isolated, directionless, with no sense of the future. It was no great stretch of the imagination.

'What are you running away from, my friend?' Walt crouched

in front of him, his voice low. The man glanced at him briefly and then fixed on a point beyond his head. His skin was grey, stretched. Didn't they get dehydrated very quickly at that age? He'd get him a cup of tea. And then what? He couldn't leave the old bugger here. Maybe he could phone the house, tip off Mrs Petrauska.

'We told the policeman.' The elegant woman had followed him in. When he looked round she was stooping towards the bench, as if she were viewing a distasteful exhibit in a museum. Fine face powder had settled in the wrinkles around her mouth. Walt got up sharply.

'Right, come on, Dad. You gave us a fright. Let's get you home.'

'So it's your father?' The woman straightened up too. She looked at him as Galen had done, like something didn't add up.

'Excuse me, I need to get him home.' He seized hold of the old boy's elbow. The man pulled away.

'Not going!' he said hoarsely.

'Come on now.' He pasted on a fake smile. 'He has Alzheimer's.'

The woman bared her teeth in a charitable smile. 'Maybe the policeman will be able to help.'

Walt pulled the elbow again and this time the man slapped him away. 'No! Coby? Where's Coby?'

'You want to see Coby?' Walt leaned in to him. The old man's unwashed smell mingled with the staleness of the old coat. The old eyes teared up; he nodded. 'Come on then. I'll take you to him.'

The man got stiffly to his feet. The woman stepped back.

Walt grinned at her. 'Panic over. Thanks for your help.' His peripheral vision flagged up a flash of hi-vis yellow coming towards him. He linked his arm through the old man's and marched him quickly through the exit.

Outside the station, the air was solid with the threat of rain, and the thunder loud and frequent. The taxi driver got out and raised a brow as Walt, breathless, manhandled Mouse's father and his Bergen into the back of the black cab.

'One too many at the Nor Loch.' He gave the driver a what-can-you-do-with-them shrug and piled in. The guy got slowly behind the wheel. More fluorescent yellow caught his eye, but it was only a workman toiling up the ramp from the station concourse. The back of the cab was roomy, with a cloying smell of pine, but he felt entombed. He was burning like a furnace under his clothes, heart hammering. Like it or not, he was going back to Stockbridge.

'Where to?' The driver turned in his seat.

'Coby,' the man said. 'Coby.'

'Cockburn Street?'

'No,' Walt said quickly. 'Saint Stephen's Church? Ssh, Mr Morrison. I'm taking you home. To Maura? Alys?'

The taxi eased into the traffic. The man fell silent for a long while, his head nodding, as if he were asleep. Maybe he had just given up. And then suddenly he jerked awake. His eyes were so lucid that Walt was taken aback.

'Alys,' he said, quite clearly. 'I was looking for Alys.'

'Why?' Walt held his breath. 'Why?'

The old man glanced once more out of the window. His gaze was distant.

36

The welcome party that greeted the fugitive was noisy and slightly chaotic, spilling out into the hall: Mrs Petrauska, all theatrical and lapsing into Lithuanian, and Mouse, pale and drawn. William, hanging back in the kitchen doorway, looked suspiciously like he'd been crying. There was no sign of Alys. Mouse grasped her father's hands and tried to make eye contact.

'We were *worried*,' she said. 'You shouldn't have gone out alone.'

The old man looked at the carpet and shuffled his feet. The dance teacher produced a heavy coat from somewhere and draped it over the thin mac, as if the man were an athlete at the end of a gruelling marathon.

Unnoticed, Walt stowed the telltale Bergen behind Shackleton. He would leave it there until things settled. The bear's great claws snagged his collar as he edged around it.

'Thanks, Walt. Where was he? How did you find him?' Mouse was suddenly beside him. The gleam in her eyes surprised him, and something other than numbness unfurled in his chest. He was glad; glad that he'd been able to do his bit, that he'd eavesdropped on two posh women at a bagel stand and manhandled her old man into a taxi. Because he would never have known the end of the story, otherwise. He placed a hand on her shoulder. No one saw, just Mouse. He clocked her sideways glance, and when she looked at him she gave a little smile, which could have been grateful, knowing, wistful – anything.

'Later,' he said. 'Tea first. The old boy must be parched.'

'Tea!' She laughed as if to say 'there you go again', and turned away from him, ushering everyone back into the kitchen.

Walt sighed and glanced up at the polar bear. It had that distant, noble, seen-it-all-before look. He told it to fuck off, before joining the others in the kitchen.

The old man had climbed out through the unlocked window in his room. Mouse was furious; she was going to lodge a formal complaint, and look for somewhere else for him to stay.

'If it wasn't for Alys,' she'd said, 'I'd look after him here.'

Walt told her not to be so daft. The old boy would fall on the stairs and crack his neck. He gave her a dozen reasons why it wouldn't work, without ever asking the burning question: why did Alys want nothing to do with her father? There were other questions too, like who was Uncle Coby and what had he done?

But what did he care? It was their shit. He had enough of his own, and any day now he was going to get the hell out of Dodge.

Mouse made the appropriate phone calls and within fifteen minutes the home manager herself rolled up in a new Audi. She had a nurse with her, all starchy and pressed. Walt almost expected them to produce a hypodermic needle like in a bad horror film.

The fight had gone out of the poor old boy. He stood up when commanded, docile as a sheepdog, with Mouse hanging onto his arm. Mrs Petrauska was fussing around him with the coat; when it slipped off his narrow shoulders she folded it neatly and laid it over the back of one of the chairs.

'You did give us a fright, Mr Morrison,' the manager cooed. Walt noticed that she didn't handle him herself, just stood back and observed. She was itching to write things down, he could tell. Any morsel of conversation that might exonerate her from blame.

'The police have now been stood down, Maura,' she said, as if this was a full-scale terrorist attack, 'though I expect they will have questions as to where he was, who found him, et cetera.'

'I expect so.' Mouse remained tight-lipped. They shuffled into the hall.

'We're going to take you back with us, Mr Morrison. In the *car*,' she said loudly into his face.

'Coby,' said the man. No one let on he'd spoken, except William, who caught Walt's eye. There was a smudged look about his cheeks. The kid had definitely been crying.

The old boy was loaded into the car. The nurse sat beside him in the back, like a prison escort.

'Better that you don't come.' The manager tilted her head at Mouse, found an appropriate smile. 'You can visit tomorrow, once we have him settled back into his routine.'

Mouse nodded mutely. The manager got behind the wheel and strapped herself in. She waved as they drove off – relieved, perhaps, that there hadn't been more of a fuss. In the back, the old man was leaning into the window, looking up at the sky. There was a lifetime of sorrow in his eyes, as if he'd lost all the good bits and couldn't quite remember why he was sad.

Mouse stood for a long time on the pavement, just watching the empty road.

'Good,' said Mrs Petrauska. 'All is well. I will take myself home.'

'Yes. Yes, thank you so much,' Mouse said.

The woman stepped lightly up the steps to the dance studio, leaving Mouse and Walt together on the pavement. Mouse turned to him. She didn't have to say anything. He held out his arms and they bumped into each other, and stood like that for a long time.

37

They sat close together on the green couch, so close he could feel the heat from her thigh, although she was careful to keep from touching him. Mouse's body language had always been pretty spiky; even now she was drinking her wine with one arm cradling her abdomen and the elbow nearest him sticking out. They'd been quiet for too long, and when they did speak, they spoke together. She said, 'Sorry this place stinks of cats,' and he said, 'It's bloody freezing in here,' and they both laughed and fell silent again.

'We could go up to my room,' she said eventually. 'I mean, it's not just a bedroom . . . It has more than a bed in it.'

He nodded, amused by her embarrassment. 'Sure. Sounds good.' He picked up the bottle and they went out into the cool hall. He followed her up the stairs, admiring her hips, and telling himself not to. This was Maura. When she said come up to my room, it was not an invitation. He didn't want to break the mood, but the mood was sort of broken anyway; a bit frayed. Maybe he needed to blow the mood right out of the water.

'Your dad was out looking for Coby,' he said.

She turned around. 'What?'

'Coby. He kept saying the name Coby. He was saying it last time, when we were in the home and he was all agitated.'

'Shit. Why didn't you say?' She resumed climbing, her feet heavy on the stairs.

'Who's Coby?'

We don't talk about Uncle Coby. A part of him didn't want to know, the part that should have been far away from here. They passed his door and crossed to the attic stair; the treads were narrow, peeking through the carpet, and the risers were plain varnished wood instead of polished teak. The banister gave slightly under his weight. At the top, he stood on a narrow landing and contemplated two white-glossed doors. He'd only been up here once, that night he'd seen William to bed. He smiled slightly at the hand-crayoned sign tacked to the left hand door: 'William's Den – Privat. Keep Owt.'

Mouse pushed open the other door. 'Come in,' she said, 'and I'll tell you.'

The room was a grown-up bedsit. An estate agent might have called it a 'studio', given the porthole window in the peak of the roof. No doubt it diffused a very classy, architectural daylight, but now it was a black circle of night. This was another window he hadn't noticed. He made a mental note to stand on the pavement the next day and look up.

Mouse had made an effort to make the place warm and cosy with pale lilac walls and yellow prints. There was a white sheepskin on the floor and a saggy couch draped in an ethnic blanket. A small coffee table bore a pile of paperbacks, a coffee mug and one of those room refresher candles in bright pink. He spotted a single bed in the corner, messy and unmade, and a pair of knickers on the floor, which she rushed to pick up and bundled into a laundry basket. He wondered whether her frantic cleaning was confined to Alys's bit of the house. Maybe Mouse could relax here, off her guard. He preferred the off-guard version.

Walt placed the bottle and the glasses on the nearest surface. He was regretting this now, wondering why he'd sabotaged himself. Human contact – raw, physical, needy – would have settled like a quilt round that guilty boulder in his belly. He had a feeling that whatever he was going to hear instead would involve more guilt, more boulders.

He didn't speak, just unscrewed the bottle cap and splashed wine into the glasses. It was cheap plonk and not very chilled. He felt suddenly weary.

They'd swapped one couch for another, but the space was smaller, more intimate. Mouse looked everywhere but at him, sipping her wine and staring into space. Her knees were pressed tightly together. *If I touch her she's going to jump out of her skin.*

'It's too difficult to talk about,' she said. 'Too hard to put into words. It's not a conversation I've had with anyone else.'

'Well, maybe it's time,' he replied.

'Uncle Coby was – is – Dad's brother. He came to live with us when I was about William's age. I don't know where he came from, or why he needed a place to stay. I don't ever remember asking, or being told. He lived in a caravan in the orchard and he sort of fitted in with us, in a way. He spent a lot of time with Dad, messing about in the shed, doing whatever men do in sheds.'

Walt smiled, remembering. 'My dad turns wood in his.' He wasn't sure if that was the right thing to say. Mouse's expression clouded and she inched away from him, like she couldn't get this out if he touched her.

'One day, Mum said he was coming to stay in the house. It was too cold in the caravan, she said, and I remember getting really upset, saying he *likes* sleeping in the caravan . . . Mum made me help make up the bed for him in one of the spare rooms.'

'No wrinkles in the sheet,' Walt murmured. 'Keep the skin in tip-top condition.'

Mouse smiled in surprise, pleased he'd remembered.

'I used to spy on him a lot. I was a curious kid, always hiding behind things, taking it all in.'

'Bit like William.'

'Yeah, I suppose all kids are like that. Grown-ups don't talk. You have to find things out for yourself. I found out more than I ever wanted to.' She broke off abruptly, and swallowed. 'He didn't bother too much with me. Alys was the . . . favourite. I tried to tell Dad about it – but my parents, they didn't want to know. They told me I was wicked, thinking like that. So Coby had the run of the place and when Alys was old enough to use a knife, he taught her taxidermy. That's where she got it from, this *passion*.'

'Obsession.'

'Maybe. They spent hours out in the shed.' She was gazing at her feet, mind far away, back in that castle. 'I would watch him, Coby, traipsing about the place. He was a wiry little man, had lots of bushy hair that made his head look big, and these little bandy legs . . . Like one of those spanners with the big end and a small end.'

'You're not selling him to me.'

'Oh, there's more. I wanted . . . I used to wish Alys would turn the knife on Coby, and we'd all be free.'

Her violence shook him. She clammed up, and he knew better than to keep the conversation going. He didn't want to know any more. She shouldn't be trusting him with her secrets.

'Oh God,' she said, suddenly. 'I'm a crap date.'

'This is a date?'

She shot him a look. 'It's kind of the end of a date, isn't it? The awkward end. At least I know you're not going to call me, seeing as you don't have a phone.'

'Maura.' He liked the way her real name felt on his tongue. He took her hand, locked his fingers with hers. 'It's late. I should probably go.'

'Probably.' She removed her hand, raised it to cup his face. She held his cheek like that, so gently, and he turned his face to lay his lips against her palm.

'But I don't want you to,' she said. 'Stay.'

'I've never met anyone like you before,' he said, and was shocked that he'd said it. She'd relaxed a bit against the cushions; her knees were still tense but her top half had a comfortable bow in it. She looked soft in the middle, pale pink top stretched over her belly and breasts. He laid his hand on her diaphragm, feeling it swell with each breath, the heat and the tautness under there. She started to say something, some smart remark, but when he looked at her, when their eyes caught, she didn't say anything. She looked young, suddenly, and vulnerable, and he leaned in and kissed her, very gently. Her glass tilted and wine splashed on his hand and they both laughed, and she said sorry half a dozen times until he took the glass and kissed her again, like he really meant it. She wound her arms about his neck, like she really meant it too.

At some point in the night, Mouse whispered, 'You'd better not be here in the morning.' They were in bed. She was hot and sticky against him, curled under his arm. For now, all the spikiness had gone from her. He liked to think he'd worn away some of her sharp edges.

'Just in case William comes in. Did you hear me?'

He realised he hadn't replied. His arm tightened around her.

'Ssh, it's okay. I'll get up early. I'll bring you up a cup of tea.'

She giggled, a soft purr near his heart. 'I can't remember the last time someone brought me tea in bed.'

He thought about that. 'I don't remember the last time I did that either.' He hugged her a bit closer. Tea in bed seemed suddenly more intimate than anything they'd done in the past few hours. And he was okay with that.

38

He stirred as the first light came creeping in through the porthole window. Trying hard to place himself, he lay rigid for a few seconds, before remembering what had taken place the night before. His left arm was dead – Mouse was lying heavily upon it, and had been for some time – but other than that, the usual aches, pains and nagging anxieties were curiously absent. A smile spread over his features. He felt fuzzy and elated, and even the act of reaching for his watch on the bedside table was transformed. He had to extricate himself gently from beneath Mouse, all sleep-warm and floppy. He stroked her hair and pressed his lips to her brow, almost hoping she'd wake up. He *really* wanted her to wake up. It was just after six, and he had no idea what time William normally got up. He'd promised he wouldn't be there come morning. And, more importantly, he'd promised her tea.

Scooting to the edge of the bed, he strapped on his prosthesis. He didn't have much to offer, but tea was one thing he could do. Getting to his feet, he turned back briefly to the bed. Even asleep, Mouse looked happy. Joy bloomed in his chest like a soap bubble. He felt washed clean, and the feeling was so sudden, so unexpected, it made him catch his breath. He wandered slowly down the stairs, trying to take in this newness. He even caught himself whistling, which was absurd. When was the last time he'd done that? Chuckling softly, he paused on the last step, in the shadow of Shackleton. The bear reared up at him in the gloom, his fur the colour of pissed-on snow, eyes slightly crooked. Shackleton had a squint? Walt had never clocked that before.

He made his way carefully towards the kitchen, noticing how the hall felt somehow odd. It took him right back to being a kid again, when you come back from holidays and the house feels cold and damp – has a distance about it. He remembered how his mam used to stand in the porch, sniffing, in case she'd forgotten to chuck out the milk, or the cloths had rebelled in her absence and gone sour. And here he was, sniffing, like his mam used to do. A house with a kid in it shouldn't feel this way. He tried to recapture the soap bubble. It had felt so good, like nothing could hurt him again. He didn't want to be hurt, and Maura and William . . . He knew he had to keep them safe.

Still puzzling over this new direction his thoughts were taking, he opened the kitchen door. He could get another job, perhaps; find them all somewhere better to live. This house didn't want him in it – he could sense its hostility. It wasn't a good place to bring up a family. The thought of family made the bubble grow bigger, wider, higher. It swelled inside him, made his whole body smile.

The kitchen was full of cats, or it felt that way. They'd just been fed and were sitting on surfaces meant for humans, preening and licking the backs of their thighs as only cats can. A heavy smell of cat food lingered in the air, and there was a presence, as if whoever had fed them wasn't far away. The hairs on the back of Walt's neck bristled. Had Alys been down this early to feed them? A quick glance at the table told him her place setting remained undisturbed, and yet when he touched the kettle it was warm. His face creased with concern, and he peered around the kitchen, not even sure what he was looking for.

He didn't want to find trouble. He wanted to be normal again. Being with Mouse had shown him that normal was still an option. Possibility shimmered all around him as he made the tea, adding extra milk to Mouse's, because she liked it that way.

He found some chocolate biscuits and arranged them on a plate, picturing her mock disapproval: *chocolate for breakfast?* He'd kiss her and tell her she was worth it.

He was grinning like a prize fool as he climbed the stairs, taking care not to spill the tea, or let the biscuits slip from the plate. As he passed his bedroom door he noticed it was open, even though he could have sworn he'd closed it. Faulty catch again? He mounted the attic stairs. Mouse's door was open too. Had he closed that? The light was on; he could hear voices. Something didn't seem right and it caught at his heart.

Mouse was awake, sitting up in bed with her hair all ruffled and her T-shirt slipping from one shoulder. William was perched at the end. There was something between them, something more than tension. There on the duvet was a black, ragged, horribly familiar shape. The rope. His rope. His mother's washing line. Mouse looked up at him with such coldness he felt something shrivel inside him.

'*You* have got some explaining to do.' Even her voice was icy. She was formidable, her arms folded tightly across her abdomen as if she was hurting there, and way too calm, staring right into him.

But when she spoke, it was to her son. 'William, go and get dressed.'

'But, Mum, I want . . .'

'William!'

'Can I have a chocolate biscuit?'

Walt handed him the plate. The kid took one and scarpered. Walt placed the mugs and the biscuits carefully on the coffee table, as if he might need both hands to defend himself. This was crazy, after the night they'd had; her in bed and him standing like a lemon in the middle of the tiny space. He wanted to close the gap between them. He had a physical need to be beside her, to seize her shoulders, make her listen to him, but she was so brittle he thought she might crack into pieces like cinder toffee.

'William found this rope,' she said. Her voice was so sharp it hurt.

'He didn't find it; it wasn't lost.'

'What sort of person carries a rope around?'

Mouse's face swam in front of him, white and intense. She looked very afraid. The truth began to filter into his consciousness.

'You think I . . .'

'Tie up little boys?'

They were both speaking together, jagged fragments that added up to something so unpalatable he started to laugh. The hollowness of it escaped Mouse; she propelled herself from the bed and slapped his face. Wincing at the sting of it, he grabbed her by the wrist before she could recoil. There were tears in her eyes, big, unshed crystals. His grip loosened, slid along the soft underside of her forearm, feeling the tension, imagining the blood pulsing beneath the skin.

'Believe me, you don't want to know why I carry a rope,' he whispered. 'But it's definitely not what you think.'

She dropped her eyes then; he was looking at the top of her head. Her hair sparked in the harsh overhead light. She muttered something that he didn't quite catch. He thought she said, 'I'm scared.' That's what she'd said in bed, and he'd kissed the top of her head, breathing in the scent of her, recognising it somehow. He was scared too. What was passing between them, it was life-altering. There'd be no going back, and it was scary and exhilarating.

'What's past is past,' he'd whispered then. 'Forget about it now.' And he'd made her forget, for a while. And now the bloody rope had been exhumed, a dark relic of a time he didn't want to think about.

I'm ashamed. That's what she was saying. *I'm ashamed I didn't see you as a threat.*

He felt wounded and pulled away from her. There was no place to go, so he just stood, with his back to her and his face in his hands. Now *she* was remembering. She was seeing in her head all those things her parents had chosen not to see. He risked a glance at her: her face was stony, the only movement a fat tear sliding down her nose.

'Tell me.' She moved forward and gripped his arm. 'Tell me what you're doing with a rope.'

'No.'

'Tell me, or I'm calling the police.'

'No!'

'I'm a single mother with a vulnerable child and a lodger with a rope. What would you expect me to do?'

'Oh, I'm still just the lodger, am I?' He slid into a chair. 'Even after last night, I'm just the lodger.'

'Let's not even go there.'

He recognised her obstinate look, the closed-down mouth that said, *I'm not going to discuss that*. And anyway, he couldn't think how to start the conversation he wanted to have. *It was special. You're special.*

'If you can't tell me . . . if you don't trust me enough to tell me, then you need to go,' she said finally. 'Just go.'

'I don't want to go,' he said, and it was the truth. 'You'd better sit down.'

39

'I tried to end it. All this stuff kept coming up, flashbacks, panic attacks. I wanted to make it stop. The things I've seen – I can never un-see them. I can't outrun what happened. I can't drown it in booze. When I got back home from Afghan . . . it was worse, somehow. Out on the frontline, you're doing something. You're *being* somebody. Back home I was just a guy who lived next to a guy who'd bought it in the desert.'

'Your friend was killed out there?' Mouse had sat back down on the bed, head bowed. She wasn't making a fuss, like his mam used to do when he talked like this. She was just listening. The old rope lay coiled, inches from her bare leg, and she'd been giving it the eye, like it was a living thing and she didn't want it creeping too close. She cocked her head up at him when he mentioned Tom, and he realised he'd never told her about his best mate, even though he'd mentioned him to William, that day he'd picked him up from school.

It was as if sharing Tom might lessen the pain, when all he wanted to do was hold on to it. The pain was all he had left of Tom, of the men they both had been. He slumped down on the couch, sucked in a ragged breath.

'Yeah, Tom was my mate. We grew up together. The Three Musketeers – Tom, Steven and me. Used to get in a lot of scrapes, believe me.' Glancing up, he shared the ghost of a smile with her. 'We enlisted together, went through basic, got posted to Afghan. He bought it on our second tour. Lost his legs. Died as they were evacuating him.'

Suddenly she was on the couch beside him, and her hand found his. It was a tiny gesture, but he squeezed her fingers until she flinched.

'Did he have a family?'

'A wife, Sara. Two little kids, and his mam and dad, of course. They still live next door to my folks. It's hard to see them . . . really hard.'

'Tell me about the rope.' Her voice was gentle, coaxing.

He glanced at the bed. 'It's my mam's washing line. Been tied to a tree since Adam was a lad, but one day I cut it down. Made a noose.'

'Oh Walt . . .' She stroked the back of his hand.

'It's okay, I didn't make a good job of it – obviously!' He tried to turn it into a joke, but it sounded hollow. He swallowed. 'Steven found me, cut me down. They carted me off to the hospital, but it's hard to patch up something you can't see. My family were gutted, but I came out all the more determined to finish the job. I just didn't want them – me mam – to have to witness it. So I took off. Left a note. Left my wallet and my phone. I camped in the hills for a while. I don't remember how long. I packed the rope in my Bergen. It was my safety valve, a constant reminder that if things got too bad, I had a way out.' It seemed like brutal logic when he said it out loud. He was scared to look at Mouse. Just when she'd made him feel good on the inside, it was all starting to come apart. She'd been right. What normal person carries around a rope?

Suddenly William's voice piped up from behind them. 'You should just get rid of it, Walt.'

How long had he been standing there? How much had he heard?

Mouse jumped to her feet, still in just a T-shirt and knickers. She grabbed her jeans from the back of a chair. 'Didn't I tell you to get dressed?'

'I am dressed.' William looked offended. 'Don't you think Walt should just dump the rope?'

'I think . . . I think that's Walt's decision.' Fully dressed, she tried to steer the kid from the room. She paused in the doorway, but the light coming in behind her made it hard to read her expression. 'Come on, let's get some breakfast. I think . . . I think Walt has some choices to make.'

He let them leave before getting up slowly from the chair. She was right. He could choose to let this destroy him. Or not. He looked at the rope, nestling in the flowery duvet, and the rope looked at him.

He made a decision.

40

Ur not the same guy any more.

The final break-up is played out in text messages. He stares at his phone, not knowing what to reply. The truth hurts. Jo has always been truthful. That's what he loved about her. Loves.

We need a break.

It was the best he could do. Wasn't that the modern way, to have a break? There'd been two days of radio silence after the station incident followed by a bleak meeting over coffee in a shopping mall. Nothing had been resolved and they'd parted awkwardly, chairs scraping back with a noise that scratched his heart. And now the texts.

Yeah. Get help Walt.

I will. I am.

Text me when ur fixed.

He is laughing at that, and the laugh comes out silently, like a dry sob. It comes from somewhere deep down. He'd thought all the raw, hurt parts had been exposed with the therapy, with all the help he'd been getting, but there's always more to discover, always something untapped, a fresh ache.

He decides that he will never be fixed enough for Jo.

41

They were both sitting at the kitchen table when he came down. William was ploughing his way through a bowl of cereal, Mouse buttering toast at the kitchen counter. Walt's heart opened painfully. Could he allow himself to believe that he was a part of this? William looked up and smiled, cheeks bulging like a hamster.

'Walt, can you help me build a Lego train today? After school?'

Walt made a noncommittal noise, looking to Mouse for approval; she usually had some excuse ready, some barrier to hand that he could never hope to get over. Now, she placed the plate of toast on the table between them and gave him a look he couldn't fathom.

'That depends.'

His eyebrow shot up. 'On what?'

'On how good you are with Lego!'

She shot him a grin and whirled away, back to the sink, picking up her cloth, wiping away crumbs. She was humming to herself. Smiling, he pulled out a chair and plonked himself down.

'I'll have you know I've served my time at the Lego yard.'

'Really?' William's eyes grew round as saucers.

'Oh aye. I've built a pirate ship and the *Battlestar Galactica*. I'm no novice.'

The kid looked suspicious. 'Who did you build them for?'

'My niece and nephew.'

'How old are they?'

'Ooh . . . bit younger than you.'

'What are their names?'

'Ella and Jack.'

'Where do they . . .'

'William, eat your breakfast. There'll be time to talk later,' said Mouse. She looked pointedly at Walt and placed a mug of tea in front of him. 'Thanks for the tea this morning, by the way.'

He thought of the two mugs, stone cold and abandoned on her bedside table, and caught her eye. Something shivered between them.

'Tomorrow morning,' he said. 'You'll get tea in bed tomorrow morning.'

Her smile made something spike inside him. William was talking but he couldn't concentrate on what he was saying.

'. . . and I always eat Maltesers when I'm building Lego.'

Walt's attention settled back on the boy. 'You mean you want me to provide the Maltesers?'

The kid nodded, his spoon in his mouth.

Walt smiled. 'It's a deal. But there's just one thing I have to do first.'

His hands were shaking so violently, he let Mouse dial the number. It was the only number he knew by heart, and he dictated it to her. She handed him the receiver, squeezed his shoulder.

'Mam! It's me . . .' He heard his own breathing in the mouthpiece, scared and shallow.

'Robert?' It was a whisper he'd barely caught. His grip tightened on the phone and something swelled in his upper chest.

'Aye, it's me, Mam.'

'Oh my God! We've been so worried, son! Here's your dad. Pete? Pete!' Her voice rose to a shout and he winced. 'It's our Robert! Steven's here as well. We're minding the bairns and he's just back from . . . What? It's Robert!'

A muffled handover, and Steven's voice came on the line, his accent as rich and broad as it had been when they were lads, before he went off to college. 'Ee, Robert! Where aya, man? We've been worried sick!'

Walt tried to smile but his mouth wouldn't stretch. 'Steven, I'm that sorry, man. I wanted to get in touch but . . .'

His mother's voice was hectoring in the background. *Is he all right? Ask him if he's all right. Tell him we had to call the police.*

'Ee, man, divvent worry. Where are ya? Am coming to get ya.'

We filed a missing persons. Tell him! It was on the news.

'No. No. I'm in Edinburgh. I'm fine, I'm just . . .'

The voice on the other end was firm. 'Stay where you are. I can be in Edinburgh by . . .'

'No, Steve.' Equally firm. 'I just wanted to let you know I'm all right. Honestly, I'm all right.'

He put the receiver down. His heart was thumping and the swelling feeling in his chest hurt.

I'm all right.

42

William was sitting on his bed with about eight boxes of Lego at his feet. Of the other boxes – the red box and the black box and the rest – there was no sign. This felt healthy. They were in the top tier of the doll's house, so cramped it was as if the walls had been squeezed together after the house was built. Walt chose a small wooden stool, painted with an image of the sun, and sat down carefully.

'I always knew the sun shone out of my arse,' he quipped.

'My mum wouldn't like you talking like that.'

Walt picked up a Lego box and examined the picture. Some kind of Mad Max automobile piloted by chubby yellow men with boot-black hair. One of them had a moustache and looked like a Colombian drug lord.

'So where's the train? Bring it on.'

William put his head to one side. 'Are you really going to help me with this?'

'Sure. I said I would.'

William's wardrobe door was a collage of frayed stickers, photographs and drawings. Miles of Sellotape glistened by the light of a forty-watt bulb. The one tiny window was pretty useless; too high up to provide an outlook, too poky to illuminate the room naturally. There was a daubed painting of a horse sitting on a rocket; another one of two females, a baby and several cats. A colour photograph of a toddler on a beach caught Walt's eye.

'Is that you? Which beach was that?'

William nodded slowly. 'I was three then, so I don't remember.'

The idea of a family holiday, of the baby William making sand pies and eating ice lollies seemed bizarre, like imagining the Addams Family on Blackpool Pier. Did Auntie Alys take Hector the stuffed cat with her, wrapped in a bath towel? He tried to visualise Mouse in a bikini; a shiny, smiling Mouse with a teak suntan and a flower in her hair. A delicious frisson ran through his body.

'Kid, I'm going to be around for a while. Bring on the Lego train.'

'But you were going to leave, weren't you, the day Granddad went missing? I saw your bag stuck behind Shackleton.'

'You knew I was planning to leave?'

The kid nodded. He was chewing his bottom lip, the way he did when he was upset.

'How? It was a spur of the moment thing.'

'I went through your bag.'

'No shit.' Walt tried to hide his amusement.

'I just wanted to find out more about you. That's when I saw the rope for the first time and I thought . . . Well, I watch the films they put on in the afternoon. There's always a man like you in them.' William had been talking to some spot on the carpet. Now he looked up, catching Walt's eye. 'There's always a man who doesn't stick around for long.'

Walt's heart contracted painfully. He tried a little humour. 'You think I'm Clint Eastwood? Make my day, punk!' He stuck out his jaw and stroked the stubble, but the joke fell flat.

'They're usually robbers.'

'I see.'

'Or murderers.'

Walt narrowed his eyes. 'Let's get back to the Lego. Trust me, kid. I'm going nowhere and I'm not planning to do anything bad. Not even to myself.' The declaration was oddly calming.

William's face broke into a smile, and he upended one of the boxes. Coloured bricks spilled out across the floor. Walt took a deep breath and picked up the instruction leaflet.

Building the train was more complicated than Walt had thought and after ten minutes he was dying for a fag. He persevered though, because the kid was obviously totally into it, correcting his mistakes and singing some funny little song.

'You never got me Maltesers,' William said eventually.

Walt perked up. 'Neither I did. I'll away out and get them now.' He got stiffly to his feet, brushing Lego pieces from his clothes.

'Walt . . .'

'Yup.'

'You know how I showed you my box collection?'

'The colour-coordinated one, aye.'

'Well, you know the black box?'

'I do. I remember the black box.'

'And I had those old photos in it . . .'

'The ones of your granddad and uncle . . .' Walt's voice tailed off. It felt a bit like Voldemort – he who must not be named.

William nodded. 'Well, when you were away finding Granddad, Aunt Alys raided my room and took all the pictures.'

Walt looked at him sharply. 'Really?'

The kid nodded. His eyes were full and watery, threatening tears. 'She took them. She said if I told anyone about Uncle Coby she would . . .' He faltered. 'If I told anyone, she'd take me down to the basement and stuff me and put me in a glass case next to the kittens.'

Walt was shocked. 'Kid, this is serious stuff. I don't think Alys is . . .' He searched for a word that wouldn't freak William out, although having your auntie threaten to practise taxidermy on you was about as freaky as it got. 'Reliable. She isn't reliable.'

'She's crazy.'

'We're all crazy. It depends how far you take it.'

'I know you *can* stuff humans. I saw it on the telly.'

'You watch far too much telly.'

'There's a college in London and the head guy asked to be stuffed in his will.'

'You're kidding?'

'Am not.' William shook his head. His bottom lip looked a bit wobbly. 'They've got him in a cabinet and they show him to visitors. They took out his organs and stuffed him with straw and wool and lavender. The head went wrong though, so they had to make a wax head.'

'Ugh, that's gross.' Walt felt himself shudder.

'True, though.'

'Whatever. She won't touch you. And anyway, why didn't you tell your mam?'

William was definitely crying now, in an angry boy way, with lots of sniffing, the tears swiped away before they could fall. 'Because she wouldn't believe me. She's afraid of upsetting Alys.' Sniff. 'And she won't talk about Uncle Coby.'

She talked to me. Walt sunk his head to his chest for a moment, pressing the heel of his hands against his eyes. The darkness cooled and sparked behind his lids. He sat upright, flexed his shoulders as if trying to shift a great weight. 'What do you know about Uncle Coby?'

William shrugged uncertainly. 'Nothing, really. But I'm sure there's somebody in the house.'

'How d'you mean?'

'I keep thinking I hear things. Doors opening. I think someone comes into my room at night.'

Walt's heart began to speed up. 'It's an old house. Things creak and stuff doesn't always work. Look at my door catch. How many times has that bad boy woken me up in the night?'

The kid had got himself into a spin and he wasn't going to be coaxed out of it. The half-built train lay forgotten on the carpet. 'And I keep smelling onions.'

'That's Mrs Petrauska and her funny stew!'

'No.' William shook his head. 'It's not.'

'I dunno what to say, kid. There's no one around, and anyway, I'm here now. How about I go and get us some Maltesers?' And some much-needed fags, he thought. William nodded and Walt ruffled his hair. 'Good lad. See how much of that train you can build before I come back.'

He turned to go. William got up suddenly, scattering Lego in his wake. 'Wait . . . I wanted to give you this.'

He dropped something into Walt's outstretched palm. It was the overcoat button, with the glinting eagle.

'Thanks, son.'

'You can keep it, if you promise me something.'

'Anything.'

'Get rid of the rope.'

Walt chucked his mother's washing line into someone else's bin on his way to the newsagent. It felt good. Liberating.

He thought about his mother, though, and the pang bit deep. She'd be pleased, wouldn't she? To think he'd taken up with a nice girl. That's what she'd always wanted, someone kind to settle him down. Mouse would get on well with his Dad, too, and Steven. Give him a bit more time and he would ring them again, arrange to meet up. When he was ready. As he walked, he imagined William sharing his toys with Ella and Jack, and it was so alien to his normal thoughts that he started chuckling, right there in the street; an old lady tutted at him like he'd broken some bylaw. He would phone them as soon as he got back. He would make contact again. He felt ready.

In the shop he bought a few cans of beer, wine for Mouse. Maltesers and chews and whatever he thought would go down well with a kid of William's age. He even bought him a comic, and flicked through it on the way home. It made him feel young again, a bit carefree.

That earlier conversation kept coming back to him though. William really thought there'd been someone in the house, and the notion of it was niggling away at him. The kid had a vivid imagination; it could be far-fetched nonsense, and yet . . . He needed to keep a closer eye on things. It was possible that Alys had some guy visiting her, some guy from the country who brought her dead offerings, like a tomcat, and that was what William was picking up on. You couldn't expect her to live like a nun, after all.

But the Coby thing was disturbing. Why would she threaten the kid? And take away the photos? Add to that old Mr Morrison's ramblings, and he wasn't liking the direction his thoughts were taking. A sick feeling began to take root in his gut, like he'd drunk a bad pint or some dirty water.

There was no sign of Mouse when he returned, but William was lolling on the couch in the sitting room, glued to the telly. His eyes tracked the screen. Some bloke in a flash suit was leading a bunch of antique hunters through a flea market.

'Chews or chocolate?' Walt held out both. William shrugged and took the chews. Walt slid the chocolate into his jacket pocket.

In the harsh light from the screen, the kid's features looked strangely grown up, as if all the boyish padding had been sucked out, leaving the straight nose and sharp chin of a mini adult.

'Where's your mother, kid?'

'She's taking a plate back to Mrs P.'

Walt wondered if he should tell Mouse about William's fears. He had no right, really, to dredge up all that stuff without some concrete evidence. When she'd spilled the beans about this Coby guy the night before, her pain had been so raw Walt felt it like it was his own.

When he and Steven and Tom were lads, Mam and Dad used to take them on trips to the coast: to Bamburgh with the knights' castle, or Craster for crab sandwiches. He remembered one time his mother had given them a huge shell she'd found on the sand.

'Whisper your troubles into it, and chuck it into the sea,' she'd said, 'and the tide will wash it up on somebody else's beach.' Walt had thought that a bit odd. Surely that meant your troubles just became someone else's problem, like weeds or litter? He went along with it anyway – although what sort of problems did you have at eight?

Last night, Mouse had poured her troubles into his ear. He'd done his best to wash over her, to sweep her up and away from all the things that were dragging her down and keeping her awake at night. The trouble was that everything would fetch up on the beach again, in the time it took you to put on your clothes, and you'd end up walking around with sand in your shoes.

She didn't like to talk about things, Mouse. William had said as much: *My mum doesn't want to talk about Uncle Coby*. She wanted the past to stay buried, but he was here to tell her it doesn't work like that. The past is alive and living among us.

The door banged and he got to his feet. Mouse's voice sing-songed through the hall. 'William? Walt, where are you?'

He was watching the door when she walked in, and that smile, the one that said she'd found what she was looking for, pierced the last of his armour.

They just looked at each other. Really looked. Mouse shook her head, and he would have taken that as a bad sign, but she was already moving towards him, unravelling, and then they were in each other's arms. He breathed in all the things about her he missed when he wasn't around her. He didn't want to move. Eventually, William could be heard making pretend-vomiting sounds and they pulled away from each other, still holding hands.

'Yuck. I hate all that stuff!' William said. 'And Mum, Walt took the rope away. Don't you think that's a good thing?'

'I think it's a very good thing.' She smiled into Walt's eyes. 'I see you bought booze as well as sweets. How about we order a takeaway, make a night of it?'

43

They spent the evening in the chilly green sitting room, eating noodles and watching an old romcom. 'I love this one,' Mouse said. 'You never see that actress in anything now.'

Walt stole glances at her profile over the top of William's head. He loved the way she gave things her rapt attention, twisting a strand of hair around one ear. She had little emerald studs in her lobes and he imagined the ice-chip coldness of them against his tongue. William yawned and sagged against him and he immediately felt guilty. Mouse looked round at the two of them. Her smile held a wistful sort of contentedness, as if she'd had a long but satisfactory day.

'Come on, toots. Time for bed.' She gave William a cheeky nudge with her elbow. 'Up you go and clean your teeth. I'll be there in a minute.'

Would now be a good time to tell her about William's suspicions? Or maybe later, when the kid had gone to bed? She was unlikely to take it well, unfounded or not, and that was the problem – he had other plans for when William was asleep. It was entirely selfish, but he'd just found her. He didn't want to lose her to some kind of maternal meltdown. He wanted the warmth of her attention on him. It was pathetic.

In the end, it was taken out of his hands. William didn't want to go to bed. He didn't want to sleep in this house.

'Why?' Mouse demanded. 'Where else are you going to sleep?'

Walt sat straighter on the couch, tensing himself for the inevitable storm.

'I'm *never* going to sleep, not until Uncle Coby's gone.'

Silence. Walt eased himself to the edge of the seat. Mouse's eyes were boring into the kid.

'What are you talking about?'

Walt waded in. 'William seems to think there's been someone in the house.'

Mouse went white. 'What do you mean?'

'It's just that . . . Well, we've all heard things in the night, doors opening and shit.'

'I have heard noises,' she said reluctantly. 'But it could be anything. Mice.'

'It's not mice.' William clamped his mouth shut and his arms over his tummy.

'William, you're just being silly. It's an old house and . . .'

'That's what I said,' said Walt, trying to sound confident. 'It's an old house and you get all sorts of weird noises.'

Mouse took William's hand with a firm *come on*. The lad was glancing from one to the other, and looked as though he might cry. Mouse placed William in front of her, driving him gently, her hands on his shoulders, thumbs meeting at the nape of his neck like a little blessing. She did that a lot. She *placed* him, like it was her responsibility to steer him safely through some imagined minefield.

Walt drained the last of his can of beer and walked after them into the hallway. William was walking up the stairs – far too wearily for a kid of eight – and his mother was standing at the bottom, sagging against the newel post, one arm hugging her belly like she had cramps. He moved towards her, rested a hand on her shoulder.

'Do you think he might be right?'

Walt didn't answer straight away. She peeled herself away from the banister and began to walk upstairs. He followed, matching her footsteps. She looked wobbly, like all the strength had gone out of her. When they came to the half landing, where the staircase changed direction, she paused and turned and they ended up standing very close together; he could smell a mixture of bleach and warm wool. He pulled her up against him, his arms full of Shetland sweater. Had she lost weight? His hands searched gently for bones.

'When you said about Dad saying the name Coby, I thought it was just memories, guilt, whatever, but . . . Maybe he's been in there, into the care home. Do you think that's why he was so agitated?'

'He's just an old guy raking over the past. Try and forget about it.'

'How can I? It's been on my mind since you told me and now William thinks there's someone here.'

They disentangled themselves and carried on up to the first floor. William was in the bathroom making lots of noise with the taps. Mouse was sitting at the bottom of the attic stairs, watching the bathroom door as if she was afraid the kid wouldn't come out. Walt squeezed himself in beside her. The nearness of her filled his head and made him giddy. He realised she was shivering.

'You're cold.'

'I *am* cold,' she said. 'It's my default setting. Every time I warm up something like this happens.' She looked at him then and he flinched at the pain in her eyes. 'I can't get away from it, from what he did to Alys. I feel so guilty.' She folded herself over her knees, as if it hurt to stay upright.

Walt laid his arm across her shoulders, and squeezed. 'Did he . . . did he do anything to you?' He hadn't meant to ask that. It came out as soft as breath. He felt her head shake and moved his hand to her hair, stroking the back of it.

'No, he didn't. He should have done. I was the eldest. That's part of the guilt. It should have been me.'

Walt's chest tightened. He thought of Tom.

'I used to see them spending time together. He was so nice to her.' She gave a dry laugh. 'He'd groomed her so well, and she was . . . Well, she was never going to see the wrong in it. That's just the way she is. I tried to talk to her about it, but she wouldn't listen.'

'You were a child yourself.'

In the bathroom, William was singing gently to himself. They listened for a time, each with their own thoughts. Mouse's face was obscured by her hair. Walt gently smoothed it back behind her ear.

'I had a book about hummingbirds once,' she said, looking up at him.

He squinted at her, not quite knowing where she was going with this. 'Yeah?'

'I knew every hummingbird fact you can imagine. I can tell you that a baby hummingbird is smaller than a penny, that the hummingbird can see and hear better than any human, and is capable of hiding the brightness of its feathers when danger threatens.'

'That could be handy, if you wanted to hide.'

She wasn't crying, but he saw her swallow the lump in her throat. 'A hummingbird's heart beats a thousand times a minute. I remember that. I had a chair in my room, an old squashy armchair that wasn't smart enough for downstairs. It was my reading chair. I had comfy cushions and a tartan rug to wrap around me when it got chilly.

'One night, I opened the book to the page with the little hummingbird and ran my finger over the shiny picture. It was every shade you could dream of – deep red, vibrant turquoise, and other colours I didn't have names for. I imagined it coming to life, flying off the page, and hovering in a corner of the ceiling like a sparkling fairy, watching over me.

'Then the door opened. It was him – Uncle Coby. He was a strange guy. He used to wear a big old army coat, summer and winter, but he always had a cold. You'd hear him sniffing. He ate boiled onions to boost his immune system, so if you couldn't see him, you always knew where he was by the smell. It would linger behind him, so you knew where he'd been and where he was heading. That was a good thing, I always thought. That you knew where he was. Anyway, this time, he walked into my room and I could smell the onions on his breath.'

Walt remained silent, trying to slow his breathing. The smell of onions. The overcoat button.

'I tried to make myself small under the tartan rug, tried to make myself as small as the hummingbird. My heart was beating a thousand times a minute.'

His heart was beating like that too, knocking so hard he thought she'd feel it.

'What happened?' His fingers stilled on her hair. He didn't want to hear what she was going to say next.

'My dad wandered past and he made up some lie and that was that. Maybe he went off to find Alys. And then he left for good, when we were still quite young. My mother said he went abroad. I was so relieved, but now, I think, what if he'd done other things, to other kids, and he went on the run? That's why I had the argument with Dad. I wanted to talk to him, adult to adult, but he still wouldn't listen. That's why we fell out. Part of me wants to talk to Alys about it but she won't. She won't talk to me about anything. Sometimes I think I'm just like . . . wallpaper.'

William came out of the bathroom, still wiping his mouth on a towel. 'I don't want to go to bed,' he whined.

Mouse got up. Walt's thigh felt suddenly cold. 'We'll stay here,' he said. 'We'll sit on the stairs until you fall asleep.'

Mouse smiled. 'Yes, we will. You don't have to worry, sweetie.' William, evidently satisfied, ran up to his room. Mouse glanced once at Walt, shyly, as if she had given too much away. He held out his hand, and she took it. His mind wouldn't quiet.

'Seriously, what if William's right? How could I not have

seen it? That makes me as bad as my parents. Mothers, we've got to be on top of everything, every minute of every day – guarding, protecting, making it all okay and if you fail . . . You know, the hummingbird is always just twenty minutes from starvation.'

He thought of her endless cycle of cleaning, of covering up. 'Nothing bad is going to happen, lass. It's okay. Go up to bed. Sleep. I'll stay here and make sure nothing bad happens.'

She touched him lightly on the shoulder, and left him sitting on the top step.

About an hour later, Mouse came out with a cushion. His hips had gone to sleep, and he was thinking he'd have to move, rub some life into his limbs, and there she was. Standing awkwardly in vest top and pants, hugging the cushion to her as if to ward off the sudden flare in his eyes.

'I thought . . . You're not going to be very comfortable out here.' She whispered it, although the kid must surely have been out for the count. His face was level with her bare thigh. She put the cushion down behind him and then, exposed, retreated a few steps with her arms crossed under her breasts. Getting up involved grabbing the flimsy banister (they didn't give a shit if it caved under the servants) and hauling; his right thigh was numb, and she rushed to support him. It was undignified but he allowed himself to play on it, teetering on his good leg and clutching at her waist until his hand found a strip of warm skin.

'You can't stay there all night. Come on.' Her breath brushed his cheek as she manhandled him around and led him into her room.

The place was dark, except for the soft peachy glow of the bedside light. She had fairy lights strung up around the bed, which he hadn't noticed last time. The duvet was unruffled, and he guessed she'd been tidying up, putting things to rights, using up her nervous energy. She was chewing her bottom lip.

'I, I just don't want to be on my own.'

'No. No, you shouldn't be.' They drew together, magnetised. The chapped skin on her bottom lip tasted of mint, and as they kissed, everything smoothed out, peeling down their bodies like hot candle wax. The bed was cold. She got into it, shivering, as he stripped off his clothes. He flung the prosthetic limb on top of his jeans. There was no awkwardness this time. No fumbling as he climbed into bed and reached for her. They fitted together as if it had always been that way. He held her gaze, and there in her eyes lay all the things she usually hid from the world. He felt it too, this loosening, this opening up to unimaginable hope. He thought the phrase 'coming home' was such a cliché, but right then, as Mouse gathered him to her, moved under him, they were the only words he could think of.

44

William's face is gaunt, waxy, like old fruit. It doesn't look like William. The mouth is misshapen, as if the teeth behind it are overlarge; his earlobes are elongated, the way they are when you're old. William has old-man ears, cauliflower ears, and that alone is enough to make Walt want to scream and yell. William was so perfect, a golden child. When Walt looks closer . . . He doesn't want to. Oh no, he doesn't want to . . . The blond hair isn't hair any more but straw: crisp, yellow straw sprouting out of the top of his head, and his eyes are staring, like doll eyes.

She got you! She got you! Walt grabs the child's arm but it comes away in his hand. Chaff falls out of the gaping wound, chaff and sand and sprigs of lavender, piling onto the floor at his feet. The floor shifts, like the deck of a ship, and Walt is slipping down, down, and William's corpse falls on top of him. He is drowning in straw. Straw smells like sand. It smells like the desert, earthy and rank.

Walt woke to thin, grey light. Had he slept? It was more like his brain had slipped into involuntary defrag mode. Images bleak as burned-out cars fused with sounds too ghoulish to remember. Dream words were lodged in his throat and he was scared he'd forced them out in his sleep: *Help! Look what she's done! Mouse!*

But Mouse was breathing softly, so he hadn't woken her. She was some distance away, but, amazingly, she was still holding his hand. It made him smile. Carefully he wriggled his fingers free.

They were damp with her sweat. He smelled of her, and his whole body soared, delicious waves beginning at the base of his belly and radiating outwards. He didn't want to leave the nest-like warmth of her bed – *their* bed – but he needed to pee, and he would check on William, make sure he was still asleep.

As he strapped on his foot, he shook away the dream residue with a determination he hadn't felt for a long time. He pulled on boxers and a T-shirt. This was a time for moving forward. He felt hopeful, for the first time in . . . He tried to calculate as he slipped silently down the attic stairs.

He'd felt vaguely glad at times, as he'd stayed one step ahead of the past. Glad of a train, a room, a lift. Of pizza when he was hungry; beer when he wanted to forget. Hopeful was a new feeling in this foreign afterlife.

He pulled at the bathroom light switch and shoved up the toilet seat. The room was surprisingly warm. Humid. He glanced around. Above the sink there was a white melamine cabinet with mirrored doors. They were misted over. He flushed the toilet and turned to wipe the mirror with the heel of his hand, as if not quite convinced by what he was seeing. Beside him, the shower curtain was drawn across the bath. His belly contracted and he whipped the curtain back; it was warm, clingy, damp beneath his hand. The great iron tub was empty, a puddle of recent water coating the bottom. The back of his neck tingled. He scanned the tiled walls. Vapour trickled down in little rivulets, pooling around the lotions and potions that stood in a line at the tap end: shower gel, shampoo, conditioner.

He stepped back. Had Alys been showering in the middle of the night? It didn't fit. Cursing, he scoured the bathroom for signs of alien occupation. He dumped the toilet rolls from their wicker basket and flipped the laundry hamper. Slightly disgusted with himself, he raked through pink knickers and socks and bloodstained shirts belonging to Alys before stuffing them back in and securing the lid. Next he opened the cabinet doors above the sink. The inside smelled of Germolene. Mouthwash, antacid, women's aloe vera shaving gel. He ran a hand through his hair and let out a sigh. What the fuck was he looking for? There were little white pharmacy boxes on the top shelf, the type you get with proper meds in, blood pressure tablets and so on. He raked them out and two fell into the sink. He looked at the labels: *Farmacia Antoja, La Rambla, Barcelona*. The name hit him like a truck. *Señor Coburn Morrison.*

He staggered back, leaving the boxes in the sink and the cabinet doors wide open. His only thought was William. If Coby was keeping his medication in the bathroom cabinet was he actually *living* here?

Hiding in plain sight.

He needed to get back upstairs and tell Mouse. They had to confront Alys, find out what was going on. Swinging round to grab the door handle, he came face to face with an old army coat. It was hanging on a hook at the back of the door, but its sinister, empty shape made him want to wrestle it to the ground. Adrenaline burst through his system. He touched the coat with the tips of his shaking fingers. It was a dull grey-blue and the last time he'd seen it was when Mrs Petrauska draped it around the fragile shoulders of Mouse's father.

Jesus. Walt seized the lapels, already knowing what he would find, muttering under his breath. *The buttons. Let me see the fucking buttons!* Two rows of imperial eagles. And the last one missing.

Fighting down nausea, Walt drooped his head for a second. The smell hit him hard, triggering a host of memories he'd put down to cooking smells or bad ventilation. All those times his door had popped open and, half asleep, he had smelled the scent of onions . . .

He used to wear a big old army coat, summer and winter, but he always had a cold . . . He ate boiled onions to boost his immune system, so if you couldn't see him, you always knew where he was by the smell.

He backed away, ice-cold sweat breaking out on his lower back. Slamming out of the bathroom, he came to an uncertain halt on the landing. Should he wake Mouse? Did he need more evidence? What more evidence did he need, for God's sake? First William's suspicions and now this . . .

Down below, he heard the front door close softly.

Walt pressed himself against the banister, scanning the empty air, every one of his senses prickling. No noise. Nothing. Had he imagined it? Silently he negotiated the stairs, edging past the great bear, rearing like a phantom out of the gloom. The hall swam with a pre-dawn unfamiliarity; concrete things wavered and reformed, ghosts at the edges of his vision. The loudest thing, the sound of his own breathing. Somewhere a clock ticked in time with his heart. Up ahead, the kitchen door was firmly closed.

It could have been any back alley in deepest Lashkar Gah: you never knew what you were going to find behind the door.

He pressed his ear against it. A faint lapping sound could be heard from inside the kitchen. Every fibre of his system was wired, his body gearing up for battle. For the first time in a long time he itched to have a rifle in his hands. The door, when he pushed it, swung open with the high-pitched squeak of a trapped animal. The room beyond was in darkness.

He flipped on the light.

On the floor beside the cooker, a hunched cat was lapping something from a dish. Walt let out his breath with a curse. Steam was rising from a pot on the hob, misting the room with the unmistakeable smell of onions. He propelled himself across the room. The cat arched and hissed, retreating to a safer vantage point. The pot was full of onion halves. Whoever had been here had turned off the gas as if they'd left in a hurry. The water was still hot, though, and the smell so pungent that Walt had to clap a hand across his nose and mouth. There was a mug of black coffee beside the kettle. Still warm.

As all the pieces of the puzzle clicked into place, revealing the full, horrible implication of what was unfolding, Walt stood for a moment in the centre of the kitchen. His hand dropped away from his face. This guy, Coby, was living here. While they slept, this monster had the run of the house, and Alys . . . Alys must know. Why else would she confiscate William's photos and threaten him like that? It was in case he went snooping and found something, or someone, she didn't want to explain.

Alys had invited the monster in.

How could he tell Mouse? Who wants to discover their sister is having thoughts about taxidermied humans and hiding a paedophile in the house?

Words crowded his head, none of them adequate. There was William's Lego train on the table, half built, lying forlornly on its side as if it had been derailed. Fresh horror hit him square in the belly. Had William been up early? Had he been down here with . . . One last glance at the steaming onions and Walt was running back up the stairs.

The curtains were drawn in William's room but Walt didn't need light to know that the boy wasn't there. There was the same absence he felt in Alys's basement; the air undisturbed by breath. He slammed the light switch, his whole body shaking from the inside out. Yellow light fanned across the bed, showing an indent in the spaceman pillow, the duvet thrown back. Walt forced himself into the room, laid his hand on the sheet. It was cold. His foot kicked something soft. William's pyjamas, one leg turned inside out, as if they'd been taken off in haste and dropped on the floor.

Shit. He searched under the bed, looking for clues that would tell him if the kid was dressed or not. No shoes were visible. Had he got dressed and gone out? Or . . . But his analytical brain had kicked in and it refused to dwell on the alternative. It was a school day. He swivelled round, eyes scanning the sparse furniture. It was a school day; there was his blue school bag, slumped against the wardrobe. What did he wear to school? He couldn't remember, and a quick search through the wardrobe gave up no information either. He'd never noticed the boy's kit, and had no idea what he might be wearing, supposing he was wearing anything.

Mouse would know. Mouse would come in here and know exactly what her son would have scrambled into first thing. She would know down to the colour of his socks. But to go in there and wake her up and tell her . . . What would he tell her? Bile rose in his throat. He remembered the first time he'd seen Tom's parents after their son had died; their horrible ashen masks of faces. He didn't want to make Mouse look like that – ever.

She rolled over when he opened the door. He could hear the rustle of the duvet in the dark and the change in her breathing that said she was awake. The room smelled hot and a bit musky, and he wanted to turn the clock back, to crawl into bed with her, skin to skin, and to wake up in a place where everything was normal. They would go out and have breakfast and read the papers and . . . His hand tightened on the doorknob.

'What time is it?' She raised herself up and switched on the lamp, squinting at him in the sudden light. Her hair was a bird's nest, sticking to bare shoulders. His body quickened with the memory of it tickling his belly. He shook away the image, came into the room and found his jeans on the floor beside the bed.

'It's after eight. I got up to go to the bog. Mouse, William is . . .' His breath caught. It was in this moment that he could shatter her with just one word. Her eyes widened a fraction. 'William isn't in his bed.'

She sat up straighter. 'He'll be in the kitchen, then?'

Walt was pulling on his jeans. It took her a second or two to register his urgency and then she was out of bed, scrabbling for her own clothes, her knickers, a T-shirt. *Oh Christ. I shouldn't have left him.* She was saying it under her breath, like a chant she'd been rehearsing for eight years, waiting for this very moment. *Fuck. I shouldn't have left him.* Her teeth were chattering.

'Coby's been in the house. William was right. I've just found his pills in the bathroom, and his coat, and downstairs . . . He's been boiling onions and making coffee, like he fucking lives here.' He touched her arm but she brushed him off. Her whole body was brittle with tension as she jammed her feet into the first pair of shoes she could find: flimsy sandals decorated with a jolly purple daisy.

'We have to wake Alys,' he said, catching her by the elbows. She tried to bat him away, but he tightened his grip. 'She knows about this, trust me.'

She sagged against him. 'No. Oh my God, why didn't I listen to William? How could Coby have got into the house?'

He pulled her after him, out onto the landing. 'I think you'd better ask your sister.'

45

The ghostly whiteness of Alys's bedroom glimmered in the dark. Long, sheer curtains played in the breeze from the open window. Mouse went for the softly, softly approach: a gentle shaking of the mound in the duvet until it stirred and messy blonde hair poked out from beneath it. Walt had to brace his forearms in the doorway to stop himself bursting in there and hauling Alys's arse out of bed.

'Alys, wake up!' Mouse shook her more urgently, 'Alys! William is missing!'

No mention of Coby. Walt's hands balled into fists. Mouse gave up on the mound with a frustrated gesture and stormed past him.

'You try. We're wasting time. I need to check his room again, and the kitchen.'

'I've already checked . . .'

'The bathroom!'

'No! Don't go in the bathroom!'

Don't go in there, and be faced with that coat, that smell. He knew how easy it was to be transported back to your deepest fears. But she was already gone, leaving him standing half in, half out of the room. A rustle from the bed, and Alys rose up, like a disturbed princess, rubbing her eyes and yawning. Softly, softly wasn't working. Walt slammed into the room and whipped off the duvet.

'Get dressed. You've got some explaining to do, but first give me the keys to the basement. All of them.'

She stared at him for a long minute. 'They aren't here, and I'm not sure what all the fuss is about.'

'Oh, you know. You invited him in, that fucking paedo, and now he's got William. I want that key *now*. The one that opens the room you can only see from the outside.'

That got her attention. She swung her bare legs out from under the duvet and Walt averted his eyes.

'I'll get them, but I have to get dressed first.'

His gaze settled on a puddle of clothes on the floor: jeans, a white bra. Alys made a shooing motion with one hand.

'Some privacy, please, unless you want to watch?'

'Piss off, Alys. This is serious. I'll wait outside.' She made him wait for what seemed like an eternity. He was forced to listen to the sounds of Mouse ransacking the house, opening every door and cupboard like this was a crazy game of hide-and-seek, and she'd soon find the kid curled up in a corner somewhere.

Eventually Alys, fully dressed, joined him on the landing. 'The keys are in the studio,' she said. Some of the blankness had left her face. He looked at her sideways as they headed down the stairs; he could see agitation in her body language. She caught his eye and something flickered uncomfortably between them. He began to regret his harshness.

'You need to help us here, Alys. Whatever history there is between you and him . . .'

They'd reached the hall and his words tailed off as Mouse came out of the kitchen. She was clutching the Lego train to her breast.

'William took this to bed with him last night,' she whispered. 'That means he's been down here this morning. He left it on the table.' Walt reached for her, and she sagged against him. 'He wouldn't have just left it and wandered off. He's been taken. Oh, Alys, what have you done?'

Dawn was beginning to seep into the edges of the sky as the three of them stepped outside. The buildings across the street loomed black; the road was still deserted. Generally Walt liked this time of day on Civvie Street. It gave him space to sit and have a fag, let the night terrors dissolve. But this particular terror wasn't going anywhere.

They hurried along the pavement and down the basement stairs. There was a light on high up in Mrs Petrauska's. Her bedroom, perhaps. Would William have gone there? He dismissed the notion – the boy had no call to run away. They reached the door of the shop. Alys kept a spare key in one of those hollow plastic stones in a plant pot. It took her a few minutes to find the right stone, sifting through pebbles and compost, and he could feel Mouse shaking beside him. Alys's fingers came away black with soil; she slipped the key into the lock and let them in.

His belly flipped over every time he entered this place. He never got used to it, seeing the dead yellow eyes all trained on him. Frankenstein eyes, animated by the flip of a light switch. He caught his breath for a second, assessing the room for anomalies. The stag's muzzle appeared moist. He'd never noticed the whites of its eyes before. It looked scared.

Walt took the lead, dodging around the counter to duck behind the curtain, fumbling for the switch on the cold stone wall. When light flooded the place, he found his gaze riveted on Alys's workbench. The huge glass case had been moved aside. He wondered if she'd finished it, but couldn't bear to look at all the little birds in their pantomime clothes. He thought of the wren, centre stage, neck distended, strung up from its own little gallows, and shuddered. Alys's tools were scattered across the bench, along with wire and tubs of preservative.

Mouse was behind him, teeth chattering as if she'd been trapped in a cold store.

'I'm going to call the police.' Her words were coming out all jerky and strained. 'We never checked round the back. I'll go and . . .'

'Wait. Let's just see.' Walt held her arm. Alys was opening the till. He'd heard the typewriter-clatter as the drawer shot out. So that's where she kept the keys, he thought. Under the change drawer.

'Don't call the police,' Alys whispered. 'Please don't.' Walt could see it now, the distress in her eyes. That dead look – he'd seen it before on the battlefield, when things go pear-shaped. The stage after panic.

'All you have to do is open the door, Alys. We'll talk about this later.'

She fumbled with the first lock. Walt took the key ring, bulging with slim brass keys, from her cold fingers. The broad padlock glinted, unbreached, and he began inserting the keys methodically. He went through each one in turn, gripping the rejects so tightly it stopped his hands trembling. He was aware that Mouse was beside his elbow. He could hear her breathing in short, panicky gasps.

'If you call the cops they'll ask questions and I'll have to tell them what happened, what's been happening.' Alys began to sob quietly, and Mouse put an arm about her, pulled her close.

'You *have* to tell them anyway, Alys,' Mouse whispered. 'It's time. He has to be stopped before . . .'

Walt finally found the right key and the padlock clicked open. With a grunt he tossed it to the ground and hauled open the door. The light revealed shelves of taxidermy specimens – the wedding of the punk kittens, the rats and the frogs – not alive, but not dead either. Their energy filled the room, a sort of unwilling suspension.

'They're not here! I'm going to call the police.' Mouse's voice was scratchy. She took out her phone.

'Wait.' Alys grasped her wrist. 'There's another room.' She nodded to the back corner.

'I've seen a light through the window,' Walt said. 'When I was outside I saw a faint glimmer, like a lamp or something.' He hadn't noticed the door the last time he'd been in here, but it would have been easy to hide; a few shelves pulled across that dim corner would do it; the door itself was dingy, a flesh-coloured wartime tint, with the paint hanging off like flayed skin. There was a little arch above it, a row of stones, crooked teeth set in a rictus. In another life it would have been a quaint storybook doorway, perhaps leading to a turret staircase or a secret garden. In this place, in Alys's basement, this place of death, there was only the prospect of *something worse*.

Something worse, with a window and a table lamp.

They stood for a moment, Mouse gripping his arm, their breath mingling in the cold. Walt fingered the keys; they were damp with sweat. There was no padlock on this door, just an old-fashioned latch, the type you push down with your thumb, and a black slit of a keyhole below it. Mouse squeezed his arm.

'Try it,' she whispered.

He moved forward. The door opened.

The room was empty.

It was little bigger than a store cupboard, but someone had been using it as a bedroom. It smelled fusty and there was a sleeping bag in one corner. There was no furniture other than a chair, but there were clothes bundled up on the floor – someone's laundry. A shirt on a coat hanger hung from a nail in the wall.

'Coby has been living here?' Mouse's face was stiff. She stared at her sister, and Alys nodded again, as if she was afraid to admit it.

Walt scraped a hand over his face, letting it all sink in. 'The question is: where is he now? Where has he taken William?'

46

They ran back through the deserted basement, up the staircase, out onto the street.

'What do we do now?' Mouse had to squeeze the words out between her teeth. 'Where *is* he? We never checked around the back.'

'The gate's locked,' Walt pointed out gently. 'You'd better call the cops.'

Alys's face went slack. 'I'm sorry. I'm sorry. Uncle Coby . . . He'd been to Dad's care home. He must have asked for our address.'

Mouse was punching numbers into her phone. 'Shit!' Her fingers were sliding across the keys; Walt took the handset from her and dialled 999. He turned away, phone pressed to his ear, the other hand scrunched into his hair. He glanced at his watch. Shit, it was almost nine. How had that happened?

'He turned up one day when you were out. I wanted him to leave,' Alys was saying. 'He said I'd be sorry.'

'Police. I need the police,' Walt said quietly. When he looked back, Alys was weeping. Mouse, dry-eyed and pale.

'This is it. This is the bad thing.'

'What is? What do you mean?' Mouse reached out and grasped Alys's hand.

'It was our secret. He told me I was his favourite, and what happened . . . If I told anybody, bad things would happen.'

Walt took a step towards her. 'You didn't do anything, Alys.

Things were done *to* you. You were a child. It wasn't your fault, and nothing bad is . . .'

'But it is! William's gone! That's the bad thing. He warned me. He's taken William to punish me, but I never told anyone, ever.'

Police Scotland. Can I take your name, please?

'Robert Walton.' He turned his attention back to the phone. 'It's about a child abduction.' He covered the mouthpiece. 'Alys, it's not your fault. You're the victim here.'

'I didn't know it was wrong.' Alys had collapsed against Mouse, allowing her hair to be stroked. 'I was a child.'

Is it your child, sir?

'I tried to tell them, Alys. Mum and Dad, I tried to tell them what he was doing.' Mouse looked sick. 'They said I was trying to make trouble because I was jealous of you.'

'No, no, it's not my child,' Walt was saying. His calmness was beginning to fray. 'The child is called William Morrison.'

Mouse stepped forward and grabbed the mobile; her fingers when they brushed his were icy. 'It's my child. He's my child. He's only eight.'

We'll get someone straight round to you, madam. Where do you live?

A door banged and Mrs Petrauska came rushing down the dance studio steps, graceful in ballet slippers and black leggings.

'You are looking for William?'

'Yes!'

'Is he with you?'

They all spoke at once. The dance teacher's dark eyes flashed from one to the other. 'I see William about thirty minutes ago, and I say to him, it is very early! Why you go out so early?'

Mouse let the mobile slide from her ear. 'He was alone?'

'No, he had a man with him. The one I see you with, Alys.' There was disapproval in her eyes, and a challenge too, as if she were exacting her own little revenge on Alys. 'You remember? He had on a cap, a young man's cap, a red one.'

'A baseball cap?' asked Walt.

'The man you said was family? I say to him, I say . . .'

'Where did they go?' said Mouse.

'William, he say, we go to the museum, and I say to him, it don't open until ten, you going to have a long wait.'

'That's where he used to take me,' Alys hissed. 'To the museum.'

Caller, are you still there? Caller?

Mouse flipped the phone back to her face. 'Yes, please tell your guys to meet us at the museum. The National Museum in Chambers Street.'

'They take a cab,' Mrs Petrauska went on. 'I had doubts but the man – he is *family*, is he not, Alys?'

Alys was shaking. 'Yes. Yes, he is. The worst kind.'

47

The taxi ride across the city seemed to take for ever, the streets clogged with people on their way into work. There'd been an awkward moment when they realised none of them had any cash. Walt was down to his last eight pence, Alys never carried a handbag, and Mouse had come away with just her phone. The driver took pity on them. Walt had spun him the story but, in the end, one look at Mouse's face had been enough to convince him. He waived the fare.

On the museum steps, Walt said, 'One of us should stay here for the cops.'

Mouse and Alys ignored him, already pressing through the glass doors. He hesitated, then, figuring it wouldn't be that hard for the cops to find them, followed them into the building. The brasserie, to his right, was fairly busy, but the entrance was quiet: just a few knots of visitors poring over maps in the low-level lighting. Mothers with buggies, a handful of pensioners in full hiking gear, students.

He spotted Alys and Mouse heading up the stairs to the main floor, and hurried after them. They were holding hands, grimly focused, oblivious to the artefacts hanging on the walls. Emerging at the top, into searing daylight, they moved into the grand gallery, with its three floors and that great arch of sky.

Mouse was breathless. Her voice was shaky and the cathedral-like acoustics made it too loud, too shrill. 'Where would he take him? Where did he take you?'

She jiggled Alys's hand, as if that would somehow release the appropriate memory.

Alys just shrugged. 'I remember the animals, the taxidermy. He used to bring me to see the animals.'

'So where are the stuffed things then?' Walt said, coming to a stop next to them on the slick marble floor. 'Let's start there.' He spun around, scanning the galleries, before asking directions from a woman with a walkie-talkie.

'Taxidermy?' She pointed to the end of the gallery. 'Right through there. It covers three floors.'

Three floors of the undead.

'Great, thanks.' He led the way, striding past a statue of some deity he didn't recognise. Behind him, Mouse was starting to panic. She should have stayed at home. What if they'd gone back there?

An enormous deer skeleton was on sentry duty at the entrance to the valley of death, its expression suitably sphinx-like. Walt paused in the shadow of its antlers and glanced back. 'We're here now. Come on.' He reached for Mouse's hand. Alys followed, as if sleepwalking.

His heart dropped through his chest. The gallery was Alys's basement on a mammoth scale. In the minimal lighting, creatures appeared to loom out of the darkness; he was afraid to look up. A small child scampered past, footsteps unnaturally loud on the wooden floor. Beside him, Mouse flinched.

A dinosaur! The child was in heaven. Walt looked up, past the bare bones of the Tyrannosaurus rex and through the mezzanine floors, where all manner of creatures hung, suspended in space for all eternity.

Giant screens, eerily green, projected images of the outside, of sea and sky and bright natural things; around them, schools of stuffed sharks and fish and porpoises were trapped for ever in mid-swim. He could see a hippo, legs akimbo; another deer with tossed-back horns. A giraffe extended its tongue to taste the toes of the visitors on the second floor. More kids, excited, noisy and smelling of popcorn, elbowed their way past, and the jolt broke something in him. All the horror he'd been trying to tamp down flooded his system. Sweat pooled around his neck, his back, and nausea rose like the tide. He gripped the nearest display case and closed his eyes. Tried not to see the things he wished he could un-see.

Mouse's mobile rang. It's the police, she said. Her voice sounded like it was coming from a great distance. He was trapped under water, floundering in one of those display cabinets. He sucked in a breath, pressed his brow against the cool glass. Air seeped from his nose to mist the pane. His lids flickered open, and through the condensation he could see a crow pulling a reluctant worm from a block of wood. It fixed him with a knowing, beady eye.

Two police officers detained Mouse with endless questions. *What was he wearing? Age? Height? It's okay, we already have someone at your house.* Eventually he could stand it no longer; he had to get out of this place. He made some kind of gesture – *I'm away to look* – but Mouse was concentrating, trying to remember the tiniest of details – her boy was wearing Batman socks and trainers with blue laces – and the weight of it was crushing her. He didn't want to leave her; it was a kind of cowardice, wasn't it? Deserting his post. Letting the fear win. He told himself he would find William. He would be the one to bring him back. He had some notion of racing round the endless floors – Jesus, he would scale the railings if he had to – and tackling that pervert to the ground. As he set off, he realised that Alys had vanished. He'd been too wrapped up in his own stuff to notice, but Alys was gone.

He was glad to return to the light airiness of the main gallery. It was like sinking into clouds, full of humanity and life. He took the stairs that led up to the next level, skirting the upper entrance to the taxidermy bit – he never wanted to go in there again. Pausing beside an innocuous cabinet of fish fossils, he pressed against the banister and eyeballed the other floors, methodically checking for clues. Looking down, he found himself above the huge deer skeleton with its branching antlers. Glancing up, he scanned every floor. According to Mouse, William would be wearing a blue hoodie. He trained his eyes to look for blue. What he saw, on the opposite side of the mezzanine, was Alys.

The lower sections of the white balustrade were covered in what looked like chicken wire. Alys was crouched down, her grip so tight the metal seemed about to bite through her skin, right to the bone. Walt wanted to loosen her fingers, pull her away, but he was afraid to touch her. Her gaze was fixed on nothing that he could see.

'There's a roof garden. Did you know that? He used to take me up to the roof,' she said. 'I was older then, maybe thirteen, fourteen. I wanted to see the animals, but he used to take me up to the roof.'

The back of Walt's neck went icy. 'Let's try there.' When she didn't move he reached for her hands. 'Come on, Alys.' Her hands were those of a statue, fingers frozen into claws around the wire mesh.

'You can look over and see the whole city,' she whispered. 'The Scott Monument, Greyfriars Kirkyard. There's a map to tell you what all the buildings are, and all the stone sculptures. You can look right down through them and see all the layers of the past.'

Rage was beginning to boil in the pit of his belly, the same rage that had been festering since he'd spotted that bastard's coat hanging in the bathroom, like it had every right to be there. 'Alys, how do you get to the roof?' He tugged at her fingers. 'We need to find him. To stop him.'

She released her grip and stood, turning to pierce him with a stare. 'He said he'd throw me off the roof if I didn't do what he wanted.'

48

Alys couldn't remember how to get to the roof. There was a lift somewhere, she said, and it was on level seven. They tried the glass elevator, which was right beside them, but that only went to level five, a fact they only found out as they glided smoothly upwards.

'Shit!' Walt slapped the toughened glass with the palm of his hand. 'We're wasting time. And what are the cops doing? I haven't seen a single cop.' He thought of Mouse, alone and scared. 'I should've stayed with Mouse.'

He slumped against the glass. The ground floor of the main gallery majestically sailed into view. He could see the god statue and a wooden canoe and . . . a man towing a small boy by the hand. A small boy in a blue hoodie.

'There they are! Ground floor!' He began jabbing at the elevator buttons. 'We'll get out here and run down the stairs!' The lift stopped, doors inching open painfully slowly. Walt grabbed Alys's arm. 'Did you see them? Did you?'

'Yes. He was taking him to the other part, to the dark bit.' She was trembling.

Christ. He scraped back his hair. 'Is that where the roof garden is? In the dark bit?'

She nodded. Her lips were bloodless. 'I can't go there again.'

'I know.' They were passing a leather couch. He made her sit. 'You don't need to. I'll go. Will you be okay?'

She nodded.

He was running through a tunnel. Faces peered at him from the walls. Dolly the Sheep. There were workmen, scaffolding. Transformation, the signs promised. He veered left. The temperature dropped and he found himself in corridors of hushed stone. It smelled ancient, like the old buildings in Afghan. There were too many corners, too many twists and turns. He kept close to the wall, avoiding eye contact with civilians. A sign directed him to a stainless-steel elevator. *Level seven. Level seven.* The intel burned in his brain.

The lift took an age to descend. Just as he was about to go hunting for the stairs, the doors swooshed open. It was empty. He stepped in. Inhaled the smell of onions.

Yes. He had them in his sights now. The elevator inched upwards, stopping at every floor, even though nobody got on board. He wanted to beat great dents in the steel walls. Eventually it jerked to a stop on the top floor.

As the doors opened, the wind took his breath away. It was the sort of gust that brought the mountains down with it, and he didn't need to see the spires and flags and rooftops to know how high up he was.

He proceeded with caution, not knowing what this man would do when confronted. The ones who threaten people – women, little kids – they don't expect a fire fight.

His vision was blocked by various structures, fire escape routes and so on. He could hear voices, a woman exclaiming at the stunning panorama, and sent up a silent prayer that they were not alone.

The rooftop was a large square expanse of decking, bordered by concrete and with a solid barrier at one end. William was standing on a plinth, staring into the sort of huge binoculars you get at the seaside. Coby was standing over him, pointing out the landmarks and trying to flatten down his own wispy hair, which was lifting in the wind. At intervals he wiped his nose on a white handkerchief as big as a tea towel. There were two other people there, a man and a woman, admiring the view. While they were there, the kid was safe. The woman grinned at William as she walked past.

'Shall we go down now?' she asked her husband.

The guy nodded. 'It's blowing a gale up here. Let's get a cuppa.'

So that just left the two of them. And Walt. He had to make a choice. Rescue the vulnerable or apprehend the perpetrator. He walked into view. Coby saw him first and automatically backed away from the boy. He held up his hands and smiled.

'Walt, this is a surprise.'

'You know who I am?'

'Alys tells me all the family news.' He smiled, as if he were a jolly old uncle with nothing to hide.

William jumped away from the binoculars. 'Walt! I didn't know what was happening! He said . . .'

'I said I'd take you to the museum, son.' The man took a few more steps backward.

Walt advanced.

'Keep going, you perv. You're nearly at the edge.'

'Now let's not be hasty!'

'I'll chuck you over the fucking edge. That's what you threatened Alys with, isn't it?'

Coby flapped the handkerchief, wiped his nose, playing for time. He scratched his scalp. He was bald on top, the remaining hair fluffing out around his ears. 'Don't take any notice of Alys. Alys is crazy.'

'Is she?' Walt laughed and took another step closer. 'And why would that be? Just *maybe* you've had a hand in that.'

'No! No hands. I never touched her, whatever she says.' The white hankie flapped in the breeze like a flag of surrender.

'She's downstairs right now, telling the cops all about what you never did.'

Coby's expression changed. It wasn't shock, exactly, but

surprise. Surprise that his past had caught up with him. Walt could see him calculating, taking stock, wondering what he could get away with. Then suddenly he broke and ran for the stairs. Walt set off after him, his heart thumping, adrenaline pumping through his veins. A cry from behind pulled him up. He hesitated and Coby disappeared around a corner.

'Walt?' William was standing all alone, looking lost. 'I didn't want to go with him. He said we could go for a ride in a taxi. I like taxis.'

Walt looked from William and back to the empty space where Coby had last been. He could still catch him, if he ran; he was faster, stronger.

'I didn't want to go with him, honest. I'm sorry.'

Sighing, Walt turned and walked towards William, kneeling awkwardly on the decking.

'What happened? Did he hurt you?'

'No. He took me to a café and bought me a cake. But it had raisins in it, and I didn't like it. And then we came here.'

Walt got up again and took his hand. 'As long as that's the worst that happened. Come on now. Let's see if we can find him.'

They ran down the concrete stairs, but Coby was out of sight. They entered the museum again and took a right, skidding to a halt in front of a huge locomotive. Walt dragged in a shuddering breath. 'We've lost him. Shit.'

'Is he gonna get in trouble? He seemed nice.'

Walt pulled at the kid's hoodie. 'Let's take these stairs.'

More concrete steps spiralled further down into the building. They found another glass elevator and took that. This one had a disembodied voice, which William kept imitating. Walt ruffled his hair.

'Jesus, kid. You gave us a fright. Your mother's going to be so pleased to see you.' A weak glow burned in chest. He wanted to get Coby, though. He couldn't deny it. The bastard was collateral damage on an epic scale. From the granddad down to the kid, all those lives crippled by the way he'd chosen to live, the actions he'd taken. All of them just going through the motions and him sneaking around, never having to face the consequences.

The elevator pinged. 'You are now at level one,' William duetted with the voice.

They found themselves back in the passage which linked the modern building to the huge Victorian one. Walt recognised the sheep's face. The great marble floor rolled out in front of them. William tried to ice skate on it. The light poured in through the roof and everything seemed peaceful.

He looked up. There was a faint babble coming from the café. Something caught his eye, directly in front and above him. He recognised the space where he had leaned over the rail, like he was on the prow of some strange ship; there were the fossil fish beyond, and the archway into the taxidermy gallery. He walked closer and saw that there were two figures up there, talking animatedly. Alys and Coby, arguing like actors on a stage balcony.

William was preoccupied with some kind of wooden boat, floating still and silent on the marble floor. He was reading the sign that said 'DON'T TOUCH' and trying not to touch it. Walt looked around. Straight ahead of him was the heavy-antlered stag; to his right, the stairs curved up to their level. Should he intervene? He couldn't hear what they were saying but it seemed that Coby had the upper hand. He looked furious, reading her the riot act, finger prodding the air, Alys standing still, miserable, arms limp at her sides.

William looked up from the boat, and spied the pair on the upper floor. 'That's Alys. And Uncle Coby.'

Sudden indecision stopped Walt in his tracks. He wanted nothing more than to race up there and put a stop to this for good. That man, that bastard, was shrapnel embedded in all their lives. But he couldn't leave the kid, not now. William was his first priority. Everything else – rage, frustration, retribution – had to be put on the back burner.

Coby was grabbing Alys's arm now, making her wince. His eyes were as flinty and soulless as the eyes in her basement.

'Walt, you need to do something,' William whispered. 'He looks really cross.'

'He's just a piece of fucking shrapnel.'

Blast material travels deep into the body. The bleeding that goes on inside, beneath the skin, is often harder to treat than visible wounds.

Suddenly Coby's gaze darted downwards, as if he sensed he was being watched. He spotted Walt and pasted on an instant, shruggy sort of smile that said, *relax, just a little family tiff.*

Walt yelled up at him. 'The place is full of cops, mate. You've nowhere left to go.'

He reached for William, tugged him along by the hand. The kid tugged right back.

'But what about Auntie Alys?'

'I'm done fighting. Let's leave him to the police. Come on, kid. I'm taking you back to your mam.'

He steered the boy away, taking the stairs at a run, down into the crypt-like entrance hall. The place was now teeming with uniforms. His path was barred by two cops and the kid was whisked away from him, as if *he* were the abductor, and he had to keep telling them, *up there, up on the balcony*, the words tripping over each other.

Having finally understood what he was saying, they ushered him into a small office. A man in a leather jacket was poring over building blueprints with a guy in a grey suit, while every so often a police radio crackled into life. And there was Mouse, listening intently to a female police officer. William was crushed against her, as if she never, ever intended to let him go. She sagged with relief when she saw Walt. Something just clicked into place when their eyes met, that instant tick of recognition. He supposed that's how normal people connected. Nothing grand. No secret. Just this lifeline. She reached out a hand to him.

'Thanks.'

The single word held an ocean of meaning. He squeezed her cold fingers in his, feeling the blood pumping under the skin.

'When I saw this one up there on the rooftop . . .' He ruffled William's hair. 'And all in one piece . . . It was the best feeling ever.'

Mouse smiled with difficulty, like her mouth had forgotten how to do it. 'Where's Alys? Have you seen her?'

After a bomb blast the dust clears slowly. Things take shape. You can assess, react, stabilise. William, still clinging to his mother, piped up before Walt had a chance to form an answer.

'Coby was arguing with Auntie Alys. We saw them. What if he gets away?'

'He'll not get away. He'll not get away with anything.' Walt patted the boy's shoulder. 'His past just caught up with him.'

He wasn't sure how much William understood. But kids are resilient. And clever. A look of understanding passed between them.

They remained in the office for what seemed like a long time. The door kept opening. Heads appeared, mouthing cryptic messages, and at one point the female officer left, returning very quickly with Alys.

She stood just outside the door, talking to a colleague. Walt heard strained voices, whispered words. *Just gone . . . can't have.*

Alys's face was like one of those masks from art therapy. Not the lurid painted ones, but the unmarked blanks. There was something frightening about it. Even a painted-on expression registered some emotion, but Alys was clearly having a hard time coping with the events of the past few hours. The policewoman was asking her questions in a gentle but firm tone. *Was she hurt?* No, no, she wasn't hurt. *Mr Morrison had disappeared. Did she know where he might have gone?* Alys looked confused, and then sulky.

'How should I know? He ran. He ran away. I want to go home. Mouse . . .'

Mouse held out her arms and they went in for a group hug: Mouse and Alys and William. Alys was the first to pull away, scowling as if the lights were suddenly too bright.

'Mouse, I want to go home. Can we just go home now?'

'We'll go as soon as we can, Alys.' Mouse turned to the policewoman. 'Is it safe? Do we have to stay until . . . until it's all over?'

'Well,' said the policewoman. 'Our officers have had some trouble locating Mr Morrison. It seems that . . .'

'What? He's gone? He can't have.'

Walt saw again Coby disappearing around the corner, imagined him vanishing into the depths of the museum, melting into the shadows amongst the rows of taxidermied relics, the only hint of his existence the scent of onions and a heavy feeling in the air. He could have chased him, on the roof, could have caught him, put an end to all of this. But he had stayed with William. It had been a new choice – the right choice.

He stepped forward and squeezed Mouse's shoulder. 'This place is in lockdown. If he's here, they'll find him. The important thing is that William is safe, Alys is safe. It *is* all over now.'

The inside of the police car smelled faintly of vomit. In the front, Walt pressed close up to the window, looking into the faces of passing pedestrians: tourists with cameras and glossy carrier bags; locals making their way to work, to college; people shopping, laughing, complaining. He felt suddenly part of it all. It was a different morning to yesterday, and a million light years separated him from who he had been when he first stared into a taxidermist's window.

William, squashed between Mouse and Alys, bounced on the back seat, exclaiming over the interior of the car. *Did it have a blue light? A siren?* The policeman driving obligingly pointed out the buttons, gave the light a quick blue spin. Walt smiled to himself. Yep, kids were resilient. Was that unspoiled, childlike part of him still curled up, deep inside? Like a mouse, or a tiny fragile bird, was your real self waiting for the right time, waiting for you to hold it up to the light, rearrange it, make it new? Maybe that's all Alys had been trying to do, make something worthwhile out of a jumble of old bones and empty skin.

Back at the museum, the cop had said to him, 'When you're ready, sir, one of us will drive you and your family home.'

Family. Maybe now he could find the strength to put the past back in its place.

He turned his gaze once more to the outside. Something white caught his attention; a man blowing his nose into a hankie. He twisted so violently in his seat his forehead collided with the glass. The driver glanced sharply at him, and in the back Mouse was saying, 'What is it? Walt, are you okay?'

He rubbed at the cold spot on his brow. 'I'm grand.' The words sounded a bit wobbly. Whoever he thought he'd seen had already been swallowed up by the crowd.

His breathing started up again. He glanced back at Mouse and smiled. He said it louder: 'I'm just grand.'

Mouse sighed. 'I can't wait to get home.'

Walt checked the faces on the pavement one last time, then turned to face forwards. He was going to find that whole piece of himself, and start to heal.

Home sounded like a really good place to begin.

ACKNOWLEDGEMENTS

Grateful thanks go to the team at Polygon, especially to my editors, Alison Rae and Julie Fergusson, for all their hard work; to my lovely agent, Jenny Brown; to the members of the Angus Writers' Circle for their support, and of course to the 'Novellers', for their friendship and encouragement. Thanks, Dad, Jamie and Calum for always believing I'd get there in the end, and to all my family and friends. Special mention must go to the service personnel whose moving journals helped me to understand Walt, and to Ollie for his insider chat.